The Show Is Over

A Circus Story

Nundy Ottinis

authorHOUSE®

AuthorHouse™
1663 Liberty Drive
Bloomington, IN 47403
www.authorhouse.com
Phone: 1-800-839-8640

First published by AuthorHouse   10/21/2009

ISBN: 978-1-4490-3433-7 (sc)

Printed in the United States of America
Bloomington, Indiana

This book is printed on acid-free paper.

The OTTINIS ! A high wire Dynasty   "The show is over!"

29th January, 2008.

I was thinking of writing my memories for a very long time but always find it difficult to start because I can't make up my mind how to go about it. In the last year, I broke my ankle then I had a heart attack and now I needed to start or, I will never start again.

I was born on 11th January. 1949 and grew up in Postwar Vienna Austria. I had three brothers and three sisters. As of today, one sister and two brothers have died. My parents, uncles and aunts passed on, leaving my mother's half brother as the only living survivor, of my uncles and aunts.

My father Otto was born in his father's circus trailer, on the 12th March 1917. My father being the youngest had one sister and eight brothers. His father was a very hansom and strong man, blond with blue eyes, a mustache and very masculine, but not tall, "a real Czechoslovakian". He was also an animal trainer and his horses performed, very elegant. One of them would count your fingers, when you hold them up and scratch with his hoof in the sand. If you show him six fingers, he scratches six times. His elephants could sit and make handstand, like real acrobats. He taught them all kinds of tricks. Dogs were also trained by my grandfather. He teaches his children, to perform on the high wire and acrobatic tricks such as headstand, split handstand and salto. He sold one of his elephants, to circus Rebernick. Elephants can remember everything you do to them and if you mistreat them, they usually take revenge. Well, apparently that same elephant grandfather sold was badly handled and got very angry one day. They could not calm the elephant and had to shoot the poor animal. It was recession time in Vienna, food was scarce and they sold the meat of the elephant to restaurants in Vienna. It was very sad. After the war, people in Vienna could still remember that delicious elephant goulash.

Otto's father had a passion for his circus, wife and children. He adored his wife; she was very beautiful with blond hair and blue eyes. She was a very good cook, motherly and nurturing. After giving birth to eleven children, she was worn out and became very ill. Otto was her baby and her only remaining child at home. He was a talented loving boy. She spoiled him and let him drink at her breast until he was seven years old, because vitamins were hard to get at that time. Being in her mid-forties with eleven children was difficult and after a period of being not to well, she died suddenly. Otto was left heart broken, when ever he spoke of her to me he had tears in is eyes. After the death, of my grandmother, my grandfather turned into an alcoholic. Otto was very worried, no mother to comfort him, nobody to turn to. After a year passed, he practiced high wire tricks on a low wire all by himself, he had great ambitions. One day, his father told him, to go and get him a bottle of rum and he drank it up, in a big gulp and said to Otto, "-the rum is finished and so is my life." His head tilted to the side, he was dead. Otto was only eight years old, when his father committed suicide. He was left an orphan.

My father oldest brother was married at the time and had six children of his own. He was in Holland, performing for the Dutch Queen. He made a lot of money and had no use for his little brother. His other brothers did not care for him, so they gave him to a farmer in a very remote valley, an aria called Waldvirtel. The farmer and his family were not rich, but Otto was lucky to have a family again, who cared for him. Life was hard for a little orphan. He had to care for the children and the cows. They admired his performing skills and loved him. My father did not get much schooling, but he was good at performing. He was often sad, when he remembered his parents and where he came from. He started to train every free time he got to become the world greatest high wire artist.

When Otto was 14 years old, his fame had reached his oldest brother. Otto was the best there was. His brother went for him and offered him a job. He was then performing for his brother.

He performed for one hour, all by himself. Otto stood on his head, danced the Viennese waltz, made the split, walked the wire bound in a potato sack blind folded, rode the bike and made the clown on the wire like nobody ever could, up to this time. Nobody could walk the wire, like he did. He was like a cat, he was totally fearless and he was charismatic. For all this, his brother paid him half a shilling a day and he had to sleep on a straw bag under the trailer, summer and winter, like a tramp but he was proud to be a performer and he became a circus star.

That is how he met Trudy, my mother, while performing for his greedy brother.

Trudy and her family!

My great grandmother, was a very beautiful woman and was a voltage rider in a circus in Hungary, she could ride as a devil jump on the galloping horse, hold on to the saddle and bridle and make a handstand, all while the horse was in gallop, she also stood on the saddle and hook her foot on the saddle strips and let her body fall, next to the horses galloping hoofs, her hair thatching the ground. She was sensational. It was middle of the 18th century and the woman where supposed to be just ladies and not ride, like men. The circus mainly performed in castles, for the very rich blue bloods. When a Hungarian count, saw her performing and fell in lust with her. Wally was a virgin and was not allowed to mingle. The noble man went to Wallis father and asked him for his daughter. He promised to keep her, as if she was married to him and also if they have a child, the child would get an education and enough money for the rest of its life. He really loved Wally and soon they had a son. The boy was pampered, just like any blue blood. He learned riding and had his own horse. He went to a very good school and later, when he went to university, he learned in the beginning, but after a wile, he became friends, with the wrong crowd and soon he was just throwing parties and pay for everything. He didn't like learning any- more, he had big parties instead and very soon became a drunk. He spends all his money and the only thing he studied were beautiful woman. When he was broke, he left Hungary and went to South America, where he was hunting poison snakes and milk them, selling the venom for good money. He was a good lucking sweet talking drunk. He stayed in South America for 15 years and went back to Europe and settled in Austria when he was 40 years old. He married and had nine daughters. They where all very beautiful, hair down to the ankles, black as raven wings, black piercing eyes, skin like snow, creek noses, hour glass figure and great legs. Eight girls where like that and one of them, aunty Peppy was not, she had a man name and dressed like an old woman and she behaved like a man, she was also strong as a man. Anyway the story goes she had a penis and a vagina, but nobody knows for shore, only her mom did. The doctors offered money if they could examine her. But she never allowed any doctor to look at her.

Back then, great grand father had a traveling theater and aunty peppy had the man roles to play and the pretty girls were what they were, pretty girls. At Easter for instance the perform bible stories, the biggest story was when Jesus died. They had a thing and always fought, before and during performing, like my great grandmother, was the king and her husband was Jesus and he would say to her, "yes yellow king" He always said that to her because of her very pale skin. That angered her and she would act as if she brings him, sponge with vinegar, on the lance, to see if he is still alive. On this day, she prepared early and had a piece of shit on her lance and put it right under his nose and he was tied to the post and could not move so he turned his head and she followed with the shit and he moaned, he could not escape the stink. That's how they make each other miserable. They hated each other. After performance, all the men wanted to meet the girls and the father, make the girls sit next to him, so he could get plenty of drinks from the adoring fans. For instance if a man would say he is a miller, he would say so am I, comrade and go on to say, because you are a miller to, I make a toast to you and so on. He made plenty toasts, every night, yes he was a character. Every Girl was born in a different City and Hedwig My Grand Mother, was born in Millstadt am Millstaettersee, she eventually, became a very good performer and the title of Hofschauschpielerin, (Court Actress) she performed for Emperor Franz Josef until she married my Grand papa.

They where the golden couple, he was rich , an Austrian born Indian Sinty,tall and olive skin ,black piercing eyes ,A turned up Mustache , broad shoulders ,in short, drop death hansome.He also was, A very talented musician. He played the Violin and other string instruments. He also was an officer in the koeniglich.kaiserlichen Austrian Army and like all officers a great horse man.

She was, petite, black hair and snow white skin.She was irresistible and always get what she wanted and then she wanted Him. Rudolf had a business, building violins in Braunau am Inn and he also was a reserve officer, of the Austrian Army, that what Rich people did in this Times.He was a great Hors e Man and had Many Arabian Horses, He had them for sport and as a means of transportation. When he married Hedwig, He sold the business and went to live with her in Vienna. He bought her a Carnival and very nice Trailers, from a Factory in Germany and the trailers where pulled by real full blooded Arabian Horses.the kitchen Trailer had hand blown widow planes and the had a big Molzer organ, next to the Marry go round, also they had a factory made, German Bootsman swing with nine swings.they made a lot of money and had it in pillow cases, the never believed in a Bank Account. Or buying Land and House.They never worried, of bad times to come around.Hedwig had a housekeeper and a Maid and never worked a Day; they had lots of money and lived like Nobles.they also dressed in elaborate fashion. The children where looked after by a nanny.they lived in there trailers, as comfortable, as other people lived in castles.

The Emperors Son the crown Prinz and his wife where shot in Sarajevo and World war one started.Rudolf was drafted, because He was an reserve officer in the Austrian Army. They had one boy and two girls at the time and Rudolf was away a lot.

Hedwig was left at home, with the children and a maid and pretty soon, both of them had adulterous affairs.Just before her second son was born she discovered having had enough of her Husband and wanted a divorce. Rudolf was away and she got infected with syphilis, she got treatment and Rudolf did not know, she got pregnant , again and when the Boy was born, they christen him also Rudolf.that was 1920.1922 she got pregnant again and wanted an abortion ,but Rudolf would never agree with that , so she Just did not take treatment , for Her illness and hoped the baby would Die.She had begun to hate Rudolf.Trudy was born blind in one eye and was Covered in abscess one of them on her middle finger.

Rudolf was livid, when he found out, but he wanted to work it out for the sake of his Children. He loved them to death. But Hedwig did not want him any more; she insisted on divorce and kept the children, so she could ask for moor money.He left the business and all the trailers for the children and a big amount of money.

Hedwig took a man 20 years her junior and married him. She was almost 40 then. She and her husband spend all the money, in less than 4 years and sold what they could and did not work, they even went to see Josephine baker, the first Striptease Dancer. After all the Money was spending, her Husband went begging that's the only thing He could do, because other than fucking, he had no skills.

When she was pregnant with her first child by john, all money was spend they had also sold the wheels off the trailers. In January 1928 there was no food and no fire wood, Hedwig was pregnant. Rudolf was in Hungary, living the single Playboy live.He had lots of money to burn; he was a very successful Gambler. The Day my mother was born; He won a pair of Arabian full bloods worth a fortune. He could not be poor ever, but Hedwig's second Husband was totally useless. And so was she.

She was pregnant again, by her toy boy and went in the hospital where it was warm and cozy. The children where left alone with no food and no wood to heat the oven lying together in bed to get warm and Rudy didn't want to go out of bed because it was so cold, so he peed in the bed and the bed sheets froze to the skins of the children, they cried because they where hungry and cold. Their tears froze to their eye lashes. Vienna was so cold the blue Danube river was frozen and this happened only twice in the last century. They had a little Dog named liddy, she started to howl and scratching on the door until the fire man came. They broke open the door and saved the children. After that their Dad came for them, for some time they stayed with him and they had good food there and good care, but they missed their bad mother and run away after awhile.

The stepdad went begging and would bring home a little food. There where no jobs in 1928.in 1930 Trudy were seven, things had not improved. Trudy went to School with a little aluminum canteen, like all poor children and get a little food, there in school, she was not interested in learning, and she was hungry all the time. Also all school children, where invited for dinner, to rich people. One day she was having dinner by a rich family and the little girl there spit in Trudys soup. Trudy stood up hungry as she was and hit the girl with her empty canteen over the head, and left for home, hungry. After that she stopped going to school and went begging to the catholic priests for food.1933 her big brother Adi started to perform with them in restaurants and on the streets and they had it ok, little Heed and Rosy where send to Hungary boxing, by there Mother and had to send money Home, every Month. This was really a form of a nightclub and they where sold there like sex slaves, by there own Mother. They where not happy and both, started to look for a Husband, to get protection from the Mother. Their Stepfather was trying to beat on the remaining Children He was Jealous at them. But Adi was stronger than him and beat the crap out of him. Adi was very good in school and went to study. He was supposed to become a Priest. Trudy learned Step Dancing, Russian and Hungarian Dancing She was performing in Restaurants and bars, she looked much older, they did not know that she was only thirteen, she was a very good Dancer. Trudy had become a very pretty Girl and people could never guess that she was blind in one eye.

As she made her own money she started to have a friend name Doll short for Adolf and he performed with Her, He came from a family of thirteen children and they where cousins to Otto, Dolls Mom was a sister to Otto's late Mother and because of Doll they became her second family. She was in fact living by Dolls Father who was separated from His Wife and Trudy had no Home, she did not want to live with her mother and stepdad. So she runs his Household for Him and He was like father to her. He always had the monkey, sits on His shoulder and went in the Coffee house, pretending to read the papers; people would say "You are holding the Newspaper upside down Mister T, so what? He would say," I can read like that."He was a comedian true and true. Often he got drunk and the monkey with him, whenever the monkey got drunk he would shit on mister T shoulder.

In 1936 Adolf Hitler was hanging over Europe like a black cloud the recession had been bad but Hitler made it all worst. They Austrians had Hitler in Prison earlier and throw him out of Austria, as soon as he was released. They know that he was a dangerous person, there was a story telling that Hitler's mother was employed, as a cleaner, in a Jewish household when he was born and the story goes that his hatred, for the Jews, stems from there. After school he sought employment, as a house painter, that could not satisfy his ambitions and soon, started to dabble in politics, after his stay in prison, he then went to Germany and there, his opportunity arose, when the Germans just loved his ideas and he get his call for greatness, to become the Worlds, biggest mass Murderer. The Austrians just called him the crazy painter.1936 some of the Jews, had the good sense and fled Austria. When Hitler marched into Austria, in 1938 people of Austria where so hungry, lots of them, raised there right arm, to salute Adolf Hitler, because he promised them food and greatness. The starving Austrians wanted to believe it was going to be better. But it got worse; all he did was to place all Jews under a very close observation and made them wear a Jewish star on there chest. Also he screened the Austrians for sick and crazy children and he would take them away from the parents, he was going to create a clean Arian Race. And he would be the leader of the greater Reich. November 9, 1938 Kristall Nacht came, the night of broken glass. That was when most people had to realize, that Hitler was a Gangster of the worst sort. The Gestapo and the Hitler youths with there jack boots and swastika arm bands, went to the Jewish, section of Vienna, particular Juden Gasse and destroyed al Jewish properties, smashed the windows and raid there homes for valuables. They arrested all Jews and made them line up by the freighter train, to the concentration camp. If they resist they kill them, on the spot. If someone was trying to help, they would go with the Jews to the camps. Lots of them died on the transport, or where shot before the left Vienna. Sons snitched on there fathers, the Hitler Youth organization had brain washed them. You could trust nobody. The listened to telephone calls and screened letters, they had a super, in every house, to watch, if there where Jews in the house hiding and what people where saying at home. People where just whispering at home. Austria had fallen into the claws of a madman.

Otto and Trudy started dating. Otto was a very hansom young man, seven Years Her senior, blond hair, blue eyes and a chiseled Chest and arms, from His hard work on the wire. He Blond and Trudy dark they made a striking Couple. Also financially the did well, Trudy earned good money with her dancing she even started to collect Gold Jewelry and Otto on the high wire was also doing well. They were inseparable and one of Otto's older cousins a brother of Doll, Rather went on double dates with, Trudy's oldest sister Henni. Not to long and Henni was pregnant and had to get married to Anton, there where big Fights, over the two of them, the mothers, did not want them together. Hedwig did not want to loose, the money maker and the family of Anton, said she was not good enough, for Him. They could not afford, to lose him, he was the best artist of the group. But they could not stop them, they got married anyhow. Two very important things happened. In 1938, Otto got a letter, from a very big Circus Family, they send a contract and a ticket to America, for Otto, because, they needed a strong man for the trope, who formed human pyramids on the wire. Otto was supposed to carry other artists on his shoulders. He was so happy, the future was looking very rosy, but Anton and another of his brothers went into a drunken brawl, with a German Marine and when the dust settled, the Marine was dead.

Anton had to run, or he would be, but in front of a firing squad, if they Nazis found him. So Trudy and Otto, help to Hide Him. When they could not find a way out for Anton, they decided that Otto, will give him his ticket to America, Anton was also a High wire Artist, not as well as Otto, but not bad. He was good on human pyramids, so Otto and Anton agreed, He go first and send for Otto and Trudy as well as Henni and her baby. As Anton reached America in 1938, Otto was drafted into the German Army. They made Him a pioneer and he was stationed for the drill in Vienna for one Year. After completing his training, he was sent to Russia! Trudy was also pregnant and gave birth to a girl, Rose on the 21 of January 1940.

Otto got leave, in March and came, home to marry Trudy. She was 17 Years old. The next day, after the wedding, Otto had to go back to the front. When he came back again, little Rosy was walking and greeted her Father. Trudy showed Rose, the picture of Otto, everyday and told her this is your daddy. She was one Year old. Otto was so happy, He had his one Family. Before it went really bad in Austria Henni left to America, together with her baby. The Year was 1941.things in Austria, went from bad to worst. Otto was in Russia and could go nowhere again. There was very little food in Vienna. Trudy had her Aunty Peppy living with her. Otto was playing Black Jack with His comrades and sends her all the money he won. So Trudy was able to help, her mother as well. Her mother's husband was also in the German Army, also her brothers

Adolf and Rudolf, Rose was in Hungary married and had a little Son, Her Husband, was a Russian musician and he was making good money in Hungary. Henni was safe in America, tanks to the help of Otto. There where no food shortages and they already had bought a little House.

Things got really bad, on the front and in Vienna, Trudys friends and cousins from the, Indian side, the Sinty (Gipsy) tribe. They lived in Austria for about 10 Centuries, none the less, they where not Considered Austrians and they started disappearing, just like the Jews. Gestapo would pick them up and you never see them again. Most of the prisoners were send, to Braunau am Inn or to Dachau. This Camps where just there to kill and destroy. Homosexuals and Jews, thief's, where also send there, if mentally disabled people would have children, they take them by birth and kill them. In the concentrations Camps, They shave peoples Hair and make mattresses out of it. the skin from People, they use to make Lamp Shades, the break out there Gold Teeth, take all there possessions, even there Close and herded them to the Gas Cambers, helpless and naked like shorn sheep's. those who where Young and strong, got a stamp with the number on the hand and had to work, very hard with very small food rations, if they got sick, then there number was up and they march them to the gas Cambers. They where called Just by this number! It was not enough to take there possessions, no they also took there dignity, and there Identity. People had no moor rights, because they where Untermenschen, (low livers) no matter who the where, the Nazis controlled every thing. Only clean Arians where wanted in the German Reich to survive. At arrival at camps, they make them strip naked and herded them into the showers, everyone was trying to hide there privet parts, with there hands, shivering for fear and then when they where in, the locked the doors and no water came out the faucets but gas. They had other prisoners, who had to load the bodies on carts and load them into the ovens; they gray smoke, from burning the body's, almost never stopped, coming out of the chimneys. Good musicians had to play every night for the officers, while they eat dinner. Beautiful Woman Often, where kept as a house and sex Slave by the officers. All the Jews and Gipsys, also homosexuals where Disposed off as they please. The concentration camps, where pure Inferno. If you lucky you die, rather sooner, than later. Unimaginable, abuse and torture, was carried out by the Nazi Pigs. At the same time they had sanatoriums, for Nazi girlfriends, to increase the Nazi population. When a girlfriend got pregnant, she had to go there and was pampered like a Queen. After birth the child was raised, by the legitimate wife of the Nazi officer, to become a real Arian, meaning a Nazi Pig. The Girlfriend got the boot and had no right to her own child. The Perverted Gestapo, did there Job well. Hell was a better place, than Austria and the Greater Reich. Hitler had become like a Good, he did what he pleases and was proud of his crazy and cruel actions, and he wanted the world to be his own. At the same time his Generals seized all the properties, of the countries they occupied and of course the Jewish gold, diamonds and money was hidden in Swiss Bank accounts, they drown the Nobles, out of there castles and there the Nazis lived. Like Kings and Queens, eating only the best foods and drink the best wines, while the rest of Europe was starving to death.

Otto had exchanged fame and happiness, for Pain and Suffering, for Him and his family. He got shot true the thighs and after recovery, he got front urlaub (vacation) and came home to recover, it was 1942 and Rose was running to him when he came home. And He was so happy to hold His little Girl. After 4 Weeks He had to go back. Trudy got pregnant again; she gave birth to Otto Junior in 11th April 1943 and must have had a boy friend at the same time, because up to now nobody knows, who is Otto junior's father? There is just a suspicion, that the Greek is the Father, because Otto junior did not look, like Trudy's husband, at all. He was a replica of Trudy. The Greek was dealing, on the black market, to get the children fed. Adolf, Rudolf and Otto where all in Stalingrad and Otto's brother Rudolf was in Monte Casino, his oldest brother was to old to fight and was the only one at home, the other six where at different places in Europe.Otto had a group of solders under him and he took good care of them, they where his family, he always went to perform on the front theater and they paid him with cigarettes. Otto and his comrades ,where going deeper into Russia.The Russians had very warm clothes and where worming there way under the snow to the German solders, with a knife in there mouth to all of a sudden leap up from under the snow and cut the Germans treats, they where so silent nobody knows that they where there. The Germans had to adapt to this. They always had to be in the ready, there was no rest and no sleep, or the paid with there lives. The Russians also had female sharpshooters in Siberia; they sat on the house roofs and in trees and from one of them, and Otto took a headshot in 1944. One of Otto's boys spots her and picked her of the roof she was Death, before she hit the frozen ground. Lucky Otto survived and was send to Germany for treatment. Before he watched, many of His comrades perish. Live was very hard in Russia stumbling true the cold, in winter having to blast the earth, to dig trenches, sleeping standing up in the drenches, holding the machine gun to his chest, always dreaming, how nice it would be at home by his children and wife. That gave Him the strength to move on, with hope to come back home. Because of that, he did what he could to survive and also made sure his friends did to. So he went to the Russians in, the fire breaks, dressed in white overalls and skies and could not be seen in the snow. The Russians know that he was a circus performer and loved him for that, any change he gets; he would go over the border and exchange cigarettes for food. Almost all the supplies like winter close, boots food and in the end ammunition was stolen by the German Generals they where very greedy and could not get enough, Otto knows all that, but he kept on fighting. He didn't want to disappear in Russia, he just wanted to survive and go back home. He also knows that if the Russians won, World War 2 Austria would vanish. Otto had a wagon and Horses and as He and His friend where driving, Otto said" lets walk a little it is so cold" and he get off the wagon, his Friend said no, I am not feeling cold, Otto did not realize, that his friend was freezing to death, until He fell of the wagon, frozen stiff. The solders were, always hungry and cold. One day Otto came face to face with a Russian solder, he had a huge gaping wound, where his belly used to bee and he was holding, his guts in one hand and the machine gun, slung over his shoulder, holding on to it, with the other hand, Otto spoke fluent Russian and told him to hold on a little, he would bring help, as Otto turned, he realized that he had, made a mistake and turned back, his machine gun in the ready, as the Russian, was about to pull the trigger, Otto was faster and killed the Russian. He never made that mistake again and killed everybody on site. Things got worst, there was almost no food just cabbage and potatoes, they had it not much better, than in a concentration camp. The hospitals where full, solders had the runs from all this bad food, the donnerbalken (latrine, that was a big post over a hole, that was the toilet, for the solders), was always full and if you take to long on it, there would be ice on your rear, in fact it was so cold that the urine froze as you urinate and almost reach your penis. In the end there was so much fighting and running from the enemy to, there where almost no time to go sleep in barracks, so you sleep for some minutes, standing in a hole (schuetzengraben) the gun in your arms. They did the best they could and when they run out of bullets, the where captured by the Russians.

Otto and the other Prisoners of war, had to line up and where, made to watch, as the strapped a German officer, between four tanks with chains and started to tear him to bits, everybody including the Russians, covered there Eyes with there hands, but not Otto. He made a run for it and nobody saw it. He found his battalion in retreat and they all came back to Germany. From there they went, to France. The French resistance was very heavy and the sabotaged the German Army, where they could, every German solder, with half a brain know the war was lost. But they had no other option, they had to go on and fight, bridges where blown up and the battles got more desperate. Otto had a motorbike and a side car on it, he became a scout. He could ride it like a devil and that what he was, a dare devil outside, but a pussy cat at home. The day arrived, where they had the bloodiest battle, in the history, of world war two. Brave solders from the allied forces and the German Army died like the flies, in hand to hand combat. The German Luftwaffe heavily bombed the beach and the stukkas flow very low and picket them off with machine guns. Most of them died directly in the water, before landing. But the Allais where very brave and strong and overpowered the German Army. In the end, the sea and beach was read, with the blood of the solders. It was the sheer horror of War. Not many lived to see the end, of World war two. Otto and a handful of his comrades did.

And then the war was over for Otto, the English captured him and his comrades. The where lucky, the English captured them, because with the Russians it's either death or Siberia. Otto and his comrades had to work on a tomato farm and all they got to eat was tomatoes, any style. But they where alive, in Siberia, they would have been death. If you like to tease Otto, just ask if he likes tomatoes, he would become like a lion so angry. I also remember visitors, wanting to talk to Otto about the war, but he would say,' I live true it and I don't want to talk about it.' Just sometimes, he would talk to me about it, but not much, just how much he despised the war and that Austria was in danger, of belonging to the Russians and they would have been, not better than Hitler.

At the same time, Trudy had her own battle, on the home front. By the time she was twenty years old, she had a three Year old girl Rose and a baby boy named Otto, the only help she got, was aunty Peppy, her mother had two children Kristy and Willy, her toy boy husband was in Helsinki. Aunty Peppy would go, begging to the farmers, outside Vienna. Trudy get regular cigarettes send from Otto and the money the Army paid him. But the money wasn't worth much; you could almost by nothing for it. But the cigarettes paid for food, on the black market. Trudy also had to help her mother, she was the only support, and her mother had, the Toy boy, send no money for her. In 1942 Trudy met a Creek man at the black market. She fell head over heals, for him, he was very hansom and charming. The made a good business on the black market. It was very dangerous, but Trudy had always food for the children and cigarettes for herself. She was dressed nice and had her hair made up. One day she went to visit a relative; she was stopped by police, because she wore lipstick and the officer said," Eine Deutsche Frau Schminkt sich nicht!" German women do not wear make up! Trudy said:" but I am not German, I am Austrian and my husband, is fighting for the Fatherland in Russia, so please don't tell me, what I got to due. That was the only thing, that could make the Austrians proud, that they where indeed Austrians and not Germans. The Germans like to eat Marmalade, so before the war, the Austrians called the Germans, Marmeladinger. In the war, this was to dangerous, to call them that, but the Austrians, had food stamps and the food stamp for marmalade was card 17 so they call the Germans, card 17, instead of Marmaladinger.

Things war going better, the Greek was a great business man. He provided security for Trudy and the children. Besides that, she did not know, if she ever sees Her Husband again, or if she and her children would survive, the War. You had to take a little luck, where ever you could find it. Trudy's trailer had so many holes, you could see the sky at all times. The bombings got worse. Trudy's brother Rudolf got violently ill, with his lungs, because, Stalingrad was very cold and not enough food to eat and everyone knows, Stalingrad will fall, sooner rather than later, So Trudy's Father Had a little bone, very small, like a seed and he asked Trudy, to help him, get that seed to Rudolf, or he could die soon. They had a real conspiracy and used pass words in Romaness, to disguise what they did. So Trudy explained all to Rudolf and sends him the seed in a letter. Nobody could detect, the seed, in the letter, it was real small, and Rudolf had to but the seed in his eye and wait, until it his eye swells up, very big. Than take out, the seed and see the Doctor, Rudy did that and all went well, the eye got so big, the Doctor did not, know the reason why and they put him on the very last transport, out of Stalingrad to Germany. Rudolf's older brother got shot in the upper leg and the two of them came back home together. Everybody left behind, in Stalingrad was destined for Doom. Grandmother wasn't too happy, she said, they come home, she wants her husband to. So she pressured her ex husband, to send a bean for her toy boy and Trudy was the go in between, again. Trudy gave her the Bean and Hedwig send it to her toy boy, to Finland. We don't know, if she gave wrong instruction, on how to use it, or if he made a mistake, he went to the Doctor and the bean was found in his Eye. He was arrested and send back to Austria, Hedwig and Trudy where arrested by Gestapo and brought to Gestapo Headquarters, at the Schottenring in Vienna. When Trudy was picked up by Gestapo, she knows, this could be the end of her. Hedwig was beaten and pulled by her hair all over the floor, the Gestapo know what she did, her husband must have told them, but they where not so sure about Trudy, she had to watch, as they kick and slap, Her mother and they asked Trudy, "is this old gipsy whore your mother"? They spoke Romanes to her (gipsy tong) Trudy went cold. Hedwig was no gipsy and did not speak that language. Trudy wondered if they read and understood what she wrote in the letter, to her brother. She know if she tell them anything, they would, just kill her, despite her heroic husband and there two children. They beat her mother true the night, in front of Trudy and asking her, how it went with her mother's husband and to tell them the truth, if she wants to live. Confess if she is a gipsy and tell all about her mother and stepfather and they will let her go.Trudy said nothing at all and she closed her mind and pushed her emotions so far away, the Gestapo could not break her. At dawn, they let her out. She just sat down on a bench and could not remember, her own name, or her address, after several hours, she said, it came back to her, where she lives and who she is.

One of the cousins talked to Gestapo and told them that Hedwig's ex Husband was in fact a Sinty ,(gipsy)and that her fist 5 children where half gipsy. All of them where arrested. Aunty Peppy stayed by the children. A Doctor came to establish the race of the grandfather, Hedwig, Adie, Rudy, Trudy, he said they where all gipsy, except Hedwig, but she was a gipsy whore and married to a coward. A verraeter. All of them where put before the court and the judge found that, the children where the mothers extended arm and had to obey to her demands, like puppets. When Trudy entered the Courtroom, her father collapsed like someone who received a stab in the heart. He knows that is was a grave mistake to involve his youngest daughter. Trudy was visibly pregnant again. Adie and Rudy as well as the father where let go, because of want of evidence. They where Heroes to the Country, grandfather was also a consultant and Advisor, to the German Army and had a very important, role to play in world war one and two. Trudy was let go to her children, because Rudy had, destroyed the letter, as soon as he read it. So there was no evidence against him and Trudy, plus Trudy's husband was still on the front and apparently the Judge was sympathetic to them. Also at this time, begin of 1944 all was so desperate, there was not much Men left, still standing. They even send fourteen Year old boys to the Front. Hedwig was send to Dachau, where she remained to the end of the war. Her toy boy was put against the wall and shot. Trudy went to him before execution. He was trembling for fear and crying. He asked her to forgive him and he send his love, to his two Children, they where in Trudys care. Now, Trudy had 4 children and was pregnant with Twins, from her Greek Boy Friend. They where a very big family, Aunty Peppy went ham stern, that means gathering food, Trudy stayed home with the children and her boy friend, was trading business, on the black marked. All the days where filled, with fear and hunger. One day, the Greek did not return, from the black market. She was looking all over Vienna, she could not find him. Trudy was totally despaired for a word of him, but it never came and after six weeks, she knows that he must be death and went into labor, four weeks early. In all the heavy bombing and black out every night, she was lucky to make it to a hospital. She had a difficult delivery as always and the babies where frail, nonetheless she went home after one week; she worried for her other children and her sister and brother, alone with her aunt. Daily bombings and not enough to eat as well, as the other heartbreak made Trudy exhausted. Her brother was very afraid of the bombs and if bombs fell on the way to the shelter, they would hide under the viaduct, or a bridge, which was very dangerous, because they bombed bridges and viaducts as well as factories. The noise was so loud; it could damage your ear drums. Aunty peppy, would carry 5 year old Rosy, Otto was a toddler, he and the 6 months old twins in a pram, plus her sister 13 years old holding on to her skirt and to Willy. If a bomb fell her brother 8 years old, would shelter, under her skirt and scream loudly for help. Aunty Peppy was scared of the bomb cellar and always walk around, with a big metal bowl, on her head, that was a bowl what you use, to make a cake wit. One day she was in a bad mood and look up on the sky, hands on her hips, saying " my live he is, the Adolf Hitler and his girl friend the Japanese Princess, the Hinsammaheija "that means, we will be death this year. But Trudy wanted to go to the cellars, no matter what, she felt safer there. So almost every day, they walked to the cellars to shelter. So one day, as soon as they hear the warning, they run to the shelter. In Vienna every house got a cellar and in first district, where most houses are from, as early as the tenth Century, these Houses got 3 and four cellars going down, that's where people used to hide, from the Turks in the Ottoman Wars. The only had, water and very little food, for one night and hoped to go home before night fall, but as soon as they reach, a bomb went in the house and the house collapsed, on top of the cellar. The sealing was intact, but the door could not open. Willy almost got crazy for fear and Trudy had Her babies to look for and Willy was worst than the babies, Rosy and Otto, where just holding on to Aunty Peppy and where not complaining, day after day the where hoping to be rescued, but after being in the cellar for two weeks, with out no food and drink, Trudy's milk had dried out and the babies died. First Cristoff and then the girl Chrisoula, Trudy was completely horrified. Not only was she morning the loss of her lover, she also lost his babies. Also the possibility was strong, that they all died in this cellar. They where thirsty hungry and desperate, but they could do nothing but wait. After the babies where dead, for a day, they where dug out, from the cellar. Trudy was morning her babies, but was thankful, that her older children and Siblings, as well as her Aunt survived, without a scratch. Vienna was not as beautiful as before the war; many houses where in ruins and an air of doom, lasted over the heavy bombed City. People picking true the dust and rubble to look for survivors and to salvage what could be salvaged. Some of the woman got Baby Prams, pushing in front of them, containing all there belongings. Almost just ruins. The smell of fear and death, hung over the once beautiful city. No more young civilian men just old men woman and children, where in the streets. The German Army was loosing the war and as the bombing got worse, most People Just fled the City. It was hopeless. After this heavy bombing and no man to help them, they bundled up the children and packed up the very little things, they had left over and took the train to St.Poelten where the hoped, to get more food and less bombing. Because this was a small city, with no Industry and mainly a farming area. The train was full. Women children and old people having the same hope as Trudy and Aunty Peppy, to keep the children alive and find a place where they could live and eat.

At about midway to St. Poelten, Trudy could see us fighter planes approaching ,and as the train slowed in a curve, told aunty to Jump, out of the train ,aunty was scared, to jump out, but she also know, from the bombings in Vienna, that something is up and that they wanted to destroy Austria. Trudy jumped out first, with the big children and aunty throwing the small ones, into her arms and at last, aunty jumped out of the train, all the other people, remained in the train. Not a moment to soon, they hid in nearby woods, they could see black tall solders, parachuting on to the train. They heard heavy machine gun fire. Trudy just know what the had done, to this People in the train and after the Solders had left, Trudy went back in to the train, the children and aunty still hidden ,in the bushes, she found everybody killed, inside the train, the brains and blood splattered on the walls, children mothers and very old people, all helpless, had died. Trudy had the shock of her Live, she could not belief, her own eyes and she had to vomit, from her disgust of what she had to see, it was horrible. How could someone be so cruel? Death women still holding, dead babies in there arms, having there Heads blown off. Trudy, thanks to her good senses, had saved her family. They where so scared that the only moved behind the trees and went on foot to St. Poelten. Trudy carrying Rosy piggyback and aunty having Otto in her arms and Kristy and Willy carry there belongings, having the little bundles strapped to the backs.This thirty Kilometers where the longest of there lives, with very little food and water and the crying children clinging to them, shaking with fear, they reached St.Poelten. There Trudy found some of her friends and an abandoned Trailer of people who where already dead. The moved in and just collapsed in a heap. After they had slept, on the bare floor, they where hungry and went to Otto's Sister, who helped them out and feed them. When they regained there strength, they cleaned up as well as they could and looked for straw bags to sleep on. Also the looked for wood and nailed a table together and some chairs. Aunty Peppy went to the farmers begging for food. As usual she found a source and paid with a little gold. Then they get the news that Austria will be, soon Invaded by the Russian Army and women should hide because they would be raped. They had jumped from the frying pan into the fire. But there was no way to return to Vienna.

Trudy did not wash her self anymore and made sure she stank, because she wanted to repel the rapists. She was so dirty she looked like an old woman. When the Russians came in, Trudy and her family, hid in a very large Luftschuz Bunker. The Russians came down on long ropes, true the small air vents and where drunk. Next to Trudy, were a pretty young woman and her two year old baby boy? One Solder approached her and asked, if she speak Russian, but she was crying and trembling. She said neponimai, that means she dos not understand and the Russian was real angry and said neponimai, nepomimai, job twoi mat (a very bad curse), jammed the gun in her mouth and pulled the trigger, ofcorse the woman was death and there was blood and brain matter all over Trudy and her Family and trembling in fear, afraid to make a sound huddled together like sheep, they where left alone after this, horrible episode.

After the first killings and rapings, the sober troops came in and they where a little better, they treated people with a lot more respect. Trudy shared all her food with her friend, but then her friend, stole a pig from a farmer and gave Trudy nothing, so aunty peppy got mad and went to a sympathetic captain, to help her. He said they don't need a whole pig and he took the pig from Trudy's false friend, cut it in half and give one half to aunty and the kids and kept the other for him self. The Cirkessen came in, that's Russians with yellow skin and slitty eyes and Trudy was real scared of them, slitty Eyes and all. They were from the Chinese Border. But they where nice to the children, Otto called them for help, when Kristi washed his hair and he asked them to shoot her, with the pushka (gun), the Russians found it amusing and always came to look for them, Otto was there pet. They never came without food. The stole it from farmers and share it with less fortunate, like Trudy and her children. They were not so hungry anymore, the Russians also make aunty to thief a lot, they always say "daway, stary sapsarrap, molocha molocha"! (Quick old one thief, plenty, plenty, or they tell her, hold out her apron and fill it with food. They where very humorous and thanks to them, the hunger was over. Trudy heard that her sister, Rose had returned, from Hungary and when traveling was save; she took her family back to Vienna. The Sisters were happy, to be together again. Roses Husband was presumably death; he was caught by the Nazis spying for the Russians. Rose had her son with her, he was the same age as little rose, five years and only spoke Hungarian, but the kids get along, anyway and he soon started to speak German. Trudy and Rose lived in the American sector and stealing was not allowed; only the Russians liked that. The Americans only wanted to make out with the frauleins and have a good time; they gave them food to, but for all the wrong reasons.

So when her half sister Kristi, found luggage with girly clothing, for her self and kept it, the military police came by them. The where going for Kristi, they could not do her anything, she was only thirteen, but her brother Willy said no, my sister, the blond, did not take that, it was the one, with the brown hair. And they believed, the little bastard and arrested Trudy. She was put on trial, where she received, a one year prison term. So things just got worst again, Aunty Peppy was alone, with the four children and she had to visit Trudy in prison. Aunty faithfully went to prison every week and stood under the window, the children could not go in, to talk to Trudy. Auntie's sister Hedwig was not heard off and was still in concentration camp. Otto was also not found. Nobody knows where he was.

Aunty loved Rosy and Otto but she hated the two Bastards of her Sister Hedwig, for getting Trudy one Year in landesgericht (prison). Finally the war was over and soon Hedwig was freed from the concentration camp, Trudys Year in Prison was also over and she came home to a Trailer full of bullet holes. A letter came from Otto, he was captured by the English, thank good not by the Russians and there was hope He would return soon. All people started the wider aufbau that mean rebuilding. Trudy repaired her trailer, with supplies the Russians gave her. Hedwig Her Mother, had a nice Apartment in the Burggasse and Otto was still suffering in England eating nothing but tomatoes, he started to perform again for the English And he got plenty cigarettes as pay. He came home in 1948 and was rich in cigarettes. They were better, than money. Money was not worth the paper, it was written on. Finally the War was over for Him. Trudy was happy; to have Otto back and they took off, where they left off. Otto arrived in Vienna in his prisoner clothes and with a big box of Cigarettes. Otto was not the young Boy, he was when He left, He hugged his Children and Wife and never wanted to let go again, they had survived. When He came back it was spring 1948 and he immediately but his High Wire Act together, he exchanged all the cigarettes, for supply to build a new Trailer and he bought a Massey Harrison Tractor. Trudy's Mother Had an Arena in Vienna's Amusement park and Otto started to perform there, they made loads of Money the first night and Trudy's Brother Rudolf, who could do nothing, put all the money in a duffel Bag and left, with his wife. After this they had enough of the family reunion and after two months in May 1948 he went on tour with His High Wire Act.

He moved the Circus Trailer and the Tractor by Train from town to town He performed 1 Hr. and Rosy 8 years old would walk on the High Wire with Him, Junior was fife and He carried Him on His shoulders and in a push pram across the High Wire. He was blindfolded and bound in a potato sack walking on the wire, he strapped bayonets to his ankles and walked, he danced Viennese Waltz, made the Split ,headstand ,rode a by sickle and He also had a military helmet and bound fireworks to it and walked over the wire with the fireworks blasting on His Head. That was not good for his hearing, he stuffed wax in his ears but still it was not enough, at the end of the act, He made the Clown and Trudy performed with Him, as the Ringmaster. They where very successful and people cried when Otto made the Clown, he was hilarious. People where happy after this trying time to get entertainment again. Almost everyone had lost someone in the War. There where lots of widows and orphans. Whole generations where wiped out.

Hochseil-Artist Ottinis
Europameister und Weltrekordinhaber 1951
Otto Schöbel

The very loud noise damaged His hearing. Otto did not pay attention, to little details as his health, he had been true Stalingrad and nothing could scare Him, having put the war behind him, his only concern was, to be a good provider, for His Wife and Children. And provide He did. Remember true Him, Trudy's Sister Henni had the richness of America, his Mother in Law Hedwig was always Getting Money to, Adi was the only one who never leaned on Him for support. Adi became Director of a recovery home As soon as the war ended and married the nurse, he had met in lazaretto, (hospital for solders) they had a severely handicapped Boy, first and then four more children two Boys and two Girls. They lived in a very beautiful house, where they had servants to.

Rudy also married in 1955 to a Eurasian Circus artiste and had a son. Rosy married a carpenter and had a small carnival business. Otto was happy, that Trudy expected another child and as fall approached, the where about to perform again for the last time before going to the winter quarters. All of a sudden the Door opens and there is a policeman, standing in the Trailer, Otto says "what are you doing here? This is not a goat pen, you need to knock and wait for permission, before you enter '! The Police Man takes out His gun and says "are you the man, who has this placards displayed in the town "?'Yes 'Otto said.'"But this dos not give you the right, to arrest my Husband '! Trudy said. And she slapped the police Man in his face and took his Gun away and His Hat and said with this Gun, You can shoot the Chickens, not my Husband. I am making a citizens arrest. The Policeman said "if you weren't a pregnant woman!" "And if you weren't such a redheaded farmers Boy.' Trudy said and marched him to the police station, with her family following. When His superior see him and heard what he did, he fired the Man on the spot and apologized to Trudy and Otto and said that he was only, to collect a fine of then Schillings. When they performed that night, the business was very brisk. After this town he put the trailer and the high wire in storage, in the country side and they moved in with Trudy's Mother, who had a very large apartment in Vienna, Burggasse this was a very elegant neighborhood. Otto made sure to bring plenty Supplies to his Mother in law. Kristy, Trudy's half Sister was four months Pregnant, at Christmas and also Rudy's Wife was four months expecting, Trudy was in Her last month of pregnancy and the whole family, was in Hedwig's flat for the Holidays.Otto brought Goose and fish, butter and milk for the Holidays, all three pregnant women Where baking cookies and passed out in the hot kitchen, the family got along well, but not for long, little Junior had a ear infection and was crying, because he had a lot of pain and there was no Doctor in the night. So Trudy's Mother tells them to leave immediately because she wanted her house to be quiet. She kept all food, that's all she wanted from them. So Otto, Trudy, Rose and Junior, running also a very high temperature stood on the Street, at two am and had to walk ,across Town to Fasangasse,Otto carry junior and Rosy was to big to carry, where Trudy's brother Rudy had His apartment. They spend the last of the holidays and there they welcomed the New Year 1949 Trudys 27 birthday, was on the tenth of January and on the eleventh, she gave Birth to a Girl Nundy. Otto was very happy; he had his freedom baby and the first child, to resemble him. They lived with Rudolf until spring and then they went out to the country side, Nundy was christened there and Otto resumed performing.

Chapter 2

2. Book
The Children grow up. From 1951 to 1987

When my memories begin it was the year 1951, summer and we where on tour in Austria as we stopped in St. Poelten where my Dad's only Sister lived, Daddy wanted to go ahead, with his plan, to make a world record, on the High Wire.

As usual Rosy Otti and I where alone, Rosy had ice cream and I wanted it to. So Rosy let me have some, but I was not used to get food like that. I was not weaned of my Mother's breast and became violently sick. Daddy had to start his record on the Wire and was on the High Wire, day and night. I remember they gave me some black tablets, witch I spit in the pocket next to the bed, they didn't know, I did that. I got so very sick; the Doctor said that I will die soon. My Mother went, to get a Professor and Daddy broke up his world record, after two days, Daddy was eating and sleeping, on the High Wire. He learned in Stalingrad how to sleep anywhere. So he would say to the audience and this is how a High Wire Artist sleeps and he lay down, right in the middle of the wire, on his back, both feed firmly hooked to the side sails. He had a little bullet cooker, right where you come out, by the roof of the house and he made scrambled eggs on the Wire and eat there; only for bathroom brakes, he would very shortly, get of the wire. He wanted to make a longer record, so no one could beat him in the future, but Daddy was afraid I could die and He wanted to save me, the Professor examined me and I became injections, that medicine I could not spit out and I recovered soon. But I remained all my live, to have poor blood. After the sickness, I did not like to eat and was very skinny. So when ever Daddy came home, his first question was did my Nundy eat? No Mamma said, so he put me in His lap and feed me, for lunch, he eat Sardines and Bread. He also makes me drink, a little swig of Beer and so, we always eat together. After supper in winter time, when he did not perform, he would take me in and cradle me in his arm. He tell me bedtime stories, like Hansel and Gretel, Snow white and the Seven Dwarfs , the big bad Wolf and little Red riding Hood, Aladdin and the Thieves, Sleeping Beauty, most times, he fell asleep, before me, so tired he was.

As I was two and a half Years old, daddy said I was big enough, to take part in the performance. He would sit me on his shoulders and strap my feet to his chest, with a Silk scarf and tell me to sit very still and always Smile at the People, so they can see, that I was not afraid, that was always, the most important thing to do, even if You are afraid, You show no fear and if You cold don't shiver, just keep smiling. He had his hands free, for the balancing stick and that's how he walked the high wire, with me. I enjoyed doing this and felt that I was very important, people applauded a lot. Rosy was eleven Years old and walked on the wire by herself and she had to learn to make the split and make a bridge on the little platform on the high wire. After growing up in the War and get only little food,

Rosy eats what she liked and became, fat like a noodle. She could not bend her back very good, Daddy got very angry with Her and beat her so bad, on her behind that she started menstruating, after that, she was so afraid, that she learned the bridge fast. Also Daddy would sit on the wire and Rosy had to step over him. He was proud that (his Grosse) big Girl was a very good artiste. Daddy was also good in balancing. He could balance a cigarette paper on his nose that is difficult, because the paper got no weight, but He also balanced, very heavy things on his chin.He would hook 24 Restaurant Chairs together and put either Rosy or me, in the middle of the Chairs and balance it on his Chin. Rosy also had to make acrobatics, like the split and the bridge. That is how He made money in Winter, just performing in different Restaurants, Mamma was performing with a very small Ring like a hula hoop, but much smaller, so small she just barley could squeeze her body true and while she did that, she also balanced, a kerosene lamp on Her forehead.

Up to now, I can't belief, how cruel our parents where, when it came to performing. The put us at danger, like other people go to preschool. Otto was 8 Years old and had to hold on to Pappas balancing stick and so He walked on the high wire, also Otto would sit in the wheel barrel and Daddy would push it across the wire.

I loved dancing and I would always dance, under the high wire, on my tip toes, pretending to be a ballerina. Mamma had a big black dog, he was a wolfs hound, he would jump off the bridge, in the middle of the goose and take one of them by the neck, sliding the neck true his mouth, or He would catch little birds, when they come picking on the ground. One day he had his food and I walked near by, all of a sudden, he bit me in my face, Mamma just barley stopped him, from killing me. Now you would think she gave the dog away? No dice she did not. I still got bite marks on my face, but are not noticeable and I consider myself lucky, not to be disfigured. We also had a big Boxer Dog, he had a very long pedigree and his name was Hasso von Brettenheim, a real nobleman and he loved us Children. Hasso was light brown and had a white star ion his chest and white socks on. He was very cute. Not so long after Mammas Dog bit me, Hasso bit the Ear of the Wolfs Hound and only then Mamma gave him away, because He kept shaking his head. Rosy had a dwarf chicken and there was the picture of my Daddy walking on the high wire atop the radio and the chicken would sit on the picture and shit on it and the shit runs down the picture on to the radio. I remember this vividly, because this always made me laugh. Most of the time, we had only animals for company, I do not know if this was good or bad for us, but I do know that our Mother, did not care for us, we grow up with very little care.

As usual Rosy and I where alone and she would ride the bicycle with me on the back, I wasn't paying attention and get my foot in the spices of the wheel, Rosy run to the Doctor, to get my foot x-rayed, she was scared, but it was just a little skin, shaved off my ankle and I have still the scar to prove it. But that's how it was, Rosy spend more time with me, than my Mother. My Mother never carried me to the Doctor.

In 1953, I was four years old; we stayed over winter in Salzburg that is the City where Wolfgang Amadeus Mozart was born. He was a Musical Genius, but the Austrians did not appreciate him and let Him starve to death. They said he was crazy and up to my days, they keep making money of him and his wonderful Music. This is typical for Austria, if you want to make it in life, you better leave Austria.

Mammas brother, Rudi moved to Salzburg, after his divorce, because He worked for the American Army as a driver and had two Sons, the where living with him and in Salzburg he had another woman where he had a baby girl with. Aunty Rose followed with her Trailers and her husband and son, as well as my parents and siblings.

Like my Mother Aunt Henni, had three children at the time, her second child was a son and he was the same age as my sister. Thanks to my Dad, they had a very good live in Florida and where owners of a nice little House there, but did not bother again, to give us a hand and let us come to America,; As was promised '. They send some care packages and Grandma Hedwig, stole all of them. Of course Grandmas, favorite Daughter Kristy and my cousin Karin, plus her Daddy, and the favorite Son Willy get Tickets to America, because they where more important than us. Wile my Dad and Mom where struggling and we had to live summer and winter in a Trailer. Thanks to my parents, all the useless bastards where in America. As a Token of appreciation, they would call my Parents beggars, behind there backs, So much for my Mothers and Fathers families. In the mean time, we still spend Summers and Winters in our Circus Trailer, when you enter the door, on the left, there was a kitchen cabinet, plus a plastic bowl on top to wash the dishes and next to it was a fold out sofa where Mamma and I slept, on the right side there was the stove, witch also provided heating in winter , our dog Hasso always slept there, with his snout on the open baking door, because it was warm and ever so often he would pass stinking wind, but we loved him any way. Next to the oven, we had a dining table and four chairs, and then there was a parting, for the actual bedroom, there was a bunk bed on the left where Otto and Rosy had to sleep on top and Papa in the lower bed.

Just before Christmas Mamma awoke me and said "tell Papa I need the Doctor. " I already know the drill. She was very ill before, with her gall bladder and had a bad case of jaundice; again she stayed in Hospital, this time, for a very long time. Children where not allowed to visit and Mamma was on a feeding tube, so she could not leave the bed, for about four weeks , so when Mamma was able, to look out the window, Rosy went with me, to stand below the window and wave to Mamma. Rosy had a big Bezel and waved with that. Papa was working ,all sorts of odd Jobs over winter and he also collected scrap metal and sold it, that was good business, because Austria was littered with metal, after the war, you could find metal anywhere. He also went Performing, but the money was so low, after world war two, the Austrians where still scrambling, to live, we always had milk powder and egg powder and the yellow cheddar cheese in the thin, a banana or apple was a sensation. Rosy had a very nice school Director and they know, we had no Christmas tree and gave Rosy a big Christmas tree, full with chocolates and ginger bread, I will never forget, how happy we where and how proud Rosy was, to bring this tree for us, in this time you could still find nice people. As long as I was a child, our Mother only gave us a tree, about three times. And of cores there were no Christmas gifts. But she would say" at least you all get food, we rarely had to eat, so you all got it much better, than we had it, we would have been happy, to have it this good "and that was here way, to deal with it. It was true, we had it much better than them, but if our parents would have, put us first, like the others did, we would grow up privileged, in America. Instead we were paupers, open to any kind of abuse. The bastards where in America and did not give a shit about us. And why do we have to have it worst, when we could have it better? There in Salzburg Mamma took me to my first movie' Cinderella' I was mesmerized. After the movie, Mamma took me to the fish stand, for dinner, I swallow a fishbone and it stuck in my throat. I remember struggling to breath. My Mother gets the bone out with her finger and after I could breathe again, I promise not to eat fish anymore.

We had all our trailers forming a circle like in the Wild West and that gave us our own court yard. All the other cousins were also in Salzburg, living with us. There where the oldest, Rosy Otto Theo Ron and little us, rob and me. I had a lots of Dolls, 2 black ones, a baby Doll and dolls looking like a princess, I always draw princesses, on every paper I found, sins I saw Cinderella and my wish was, I would be a princess, growing up in a castle. Uncle Rudy brought us all the Mickey Mouse cartoons and we enjoyed reading them, when none of us spoke English. Non the less, we liked to beg the American solders, for chewing gum and would sit on the log heap, calling out to them "please give me chewing gum !" witch we always get. The big children had some tents and did not let us, small ones in. I being the leader of the little ones always bug, the big children to let us in, but they said, no babies allowed. So we left and played Doctor. I was the Doctor and I regularly, examined all the smaller children, I had four of them,lie down on the bed and examined them, penises and vaginas, I also told them what medicine to take, just like a Doctor. Looks like we got into trouble regularly. Rosy fell in a bomb crater and broke her left ankle. She had to get a cast. Uncle Rudy was divorced and enrolled Ronald and rob in the kindergarten, because He had to Work and mamma did the same to me, when she came home, from the hospital, but She wasn't working.Apparently She just wanted to get rid of Me. I wanted to be with my cousins, but the put me, with strangers and after catching head lice, Mamma sat with me for hours, with a special comp, to get the lice off my head. I was allowed to stay home again. Boy was I happy.

Mamma and her friends make me fight with the other children and I always won. They had a lot of fun with that. They called me the white devil, because my hair was white. I also had a friend, his name was Mario, he was very pretty, blond curls and big blue eyes, and he looked like an angel. Almost every Day he ask my Mother, for my hand in marriage. Mamma would say," how will you provide for her"? And Mario would say, he will collect metal and sell it. So any time he asks he would get my Hand. I met Him again, thirty Years after and he still liked me, I don't' know why.

Rosy cut off, her cast by her self, because it was itching. Mamma did not bother, to bring her back to a Doctor and her ankle, never heal proper and remain bad, true her Live. Daddy Build a trailer in spring and before the Roof was on, we already moved in, I remember lying in bed and seeing the Stars, I found it rather interesting. Everybody was starting to practice, also Mammas brother Rudy, I don't' know why, because he had no talent, everybody know that. Grandma went to Florida, to visit with Her rich and famous daughter, the one my parents help to escape there, they had a big problem, Mammas oldest sister was big pregnant, with twins, when Anna who was 16 at the time and was not only a very extremely beautiful exotic looking Girl, she was also the superstar of the family. She was the only one in the world, who could perform a contra balance, that is her father and one of his cousins where walking on the wire and where connected, true two poles, which where hooked, from shoulder to shoulder and Anna was standing on the poles, facing the other direction, away from the High wire. She had a deadly high wire accident, or so we was thinking at the time, but Years later, I learned the truth and the truth was that Anton, had not brought us to the states, because my Daddy would have upstaged Him, send just for his relatives to come to America, because non of them could do what he did, he was the best of his family and my daddy was the best of anywhere. One of them molested Anna and she complained to her father and instead of helping her, he helped his cousin and Anna, was very badly Hurt by this and called her Mother in Florida to tell her, that she made out Her live insurances, to her little Brother and also told her what her dad did to her and that she will jump of the High Wire, Anna put the Phone down and did what She just told her. She jumped and was dead instant. They where so ashamed they had killed there own Daughter, they said nothing to nobody, but at home when they where fighting Aunty always called him a killer and that what he was. My cousin told me about it. That's the Girl, who was borne shortly after her sisters dead.

When Grandma came back from Florida, she brought me a very ugly china Doll, she was taller than me, as soon as Grandma went back to Vienna, and we chopped up the Doll and uncle Rudy was juggling with her limps. Now that was fun, give something back to Grandma. The Boys went out and Hasso our Dog runs behind them. Otto did not see Him, until he was across the street sniffing a female, Otty made the mistake to call him and Hasso turned around, strait into an American Jeep and our Hasso were dead, this was the first time we had a brush with Dead, and we cried for Him a lot.

I always went to aunty Rosés Trailer, watching her making paper flours, but I found out, she did not like me she would say Nundy com in. Sit here and when I dry and sit, she would pull the little chair, from under me and I fall to the Ground, so I know I was not welcome and stop going by her.

Not long after that, all the big People, had a huge fight, they went after each other, with Sabers from world war one, real antics even at this time, but nobody get hurt and the families broke up for good. After that we went on tour alone. Grandmother would just come, once in a blue moon, to rip my parents off. She would say I am the mother and I can Say and do what I want, you all need to respect me and so it was all the time.

Rosy got a Goose that summer we had no Dog anymore and the Goose was Just like a Dog. She sits under the Trailer steps and nobody could go up, she would bite. The Goose would sit and watch our Daddy perform and when the people clap, she would flap her wings and make a lot of noise, she also went swimming with us that was great fun we had with the goose. Also once in a wile Grandfather would come and take us fishing, I always remember Him, being stern but gently, showing me things like fishing and catching a hedge Hog and cocking it for me on an open fire, even now I remember the taste, like a barbecue.

Daddy was spanning the High Wire, from Roof to Roof across the street and you have to come out, to the wire by a very small window, in the roof, normally he would make a platform and a handrail, to hold on to when you come out the roof, but this day He did not and Rosy came out from the Roof and the only hold on she found, was a live wire which shocked her and she tumbled down the roof, she was a very good Artiste, at the time, but She also, was only thirteen Years old. As she fell, the audience screamed Mamma screamed, I was scared and Papa was on the other side of the wire, he throw down his balancing stick and run across, fast as lightning and the moment Rosy get couth, in the spouting Daddy had hold on her. This was the first time, I see my Mother real angry, because Daddy was very careless, and never considering that rosy was a child and not as good an artiste as he. Also the electricity would have thrown anyone down and there was no net to fall in to. If rosy would fall on the cobble stones from 3rd floor she would have been dead or badly hurt that's for sure. After performance was over, Mamma hit Daddy with the frying pan and he did not say one word. She said she will kill him, if anything happens to her children. That was the only time she stud firmly up to him no matter what.

As I turned six, I had to go to school and this complicated my live a lot. I had to go to a different school every week and the Teacher, always would Say "children we have a new girl here, for a week, she is a High wire artiste, performing in our town for a week. "After the introduction, they would ask me some Questions, like "aren't you afraid and what is it like? Well I was not afraid, but it was very pain full, not to have any friends and always being told, not to mix with privet people. Just stay with your family. But I did not talk about this to no one. If we where lucky we would have our trailer, over winter, in Vienna next to where mammas Sinty cousins had there property. They where all in concentration camp and after they where freed, they where rich, they all get a reparation pension and had ten Years tax free ,on top of that they all had business. They where selling hand made Persian rugs, and some where Horse dealers, there was fife families living on the same compound. Those cousins, who where my mammas age or older, had the tattoo on there hand, with the prisoners number, C my Grandmother had that to.)and because the where in the camp, when they where children, they could not Wright or read, but all of them know, how to count money very well, one of them had a chauffeur, for his Mercedes Benz, because if you illiterate, You can not obtain a drivers permit in Austria and he was traveling true Austria to sell his rugs, he had gold faucets in his bathroom and thick Persian rugs, true out his House ,every morning, when they went to the café, for breakfast, he would tell the chauffeur, 'come and read me the paper, I forget my reading glasses!' so nobody knows, he could not read. The where nice and Lilly, mammas cousin, would cook, lots of food everyday, so you could always drop in and get food, everyday was a party there, they also had children our age and that where our friends. We had electricity from them, but when we woke up, in the morning to go to school, it was bitter cold in the trailer and wile Otto made a fire in the oven, I stood on the chair next to the oven, to dress, because higher up it is warmer fast, when I put on my stockings, I stumbled and fell, I stretched out my hands and fell with my hands, on the red hot stove. I moved quickly away from it, otherwise my hands would ketch fire, there was the water pocket, next to the oven and I went with my hands in the ice cold water and stayed there for a very long time, I could not hold a pen for weeks, my mother did not bother to bring me to a doctor..

We played Indians and cowboy after school and when spring came around, we practiced. I had a little dog name buzi and I loved this dog, one day I came home from school, my dog was not here, turns out, my mother sold my buzi, to an old lady, the only good thing about it, Buzi had a very good live with her. Then it was time to go on tour and we where not happy, to live our cousins.

In summer, Rosy, Otto and I where always together, moving from town to town, practicing and performing. Otto was very slender, but had lots of mussels, from all the hard work. He already had to help, put up the high wire and besides that he, was already performing, like a grown man. He could walk up on the tail of the high wire; witch had a steep incline, with out a balancing stick, when he was twelve years old. I was very proud that he was my big brother. Otto was very protective of Rosy and I and he would even beat, much bigger boys than he was, if they interfere with us. One day a grown man, wanted to be fresh with Rosy and Otto heard it, he Just went to the man and jumped up, because the man was much taller than him and hit the man an upper cut and then run away, because if they would ketch him, that would have been danger. This winter when I went school we where in Vienna having our trailers parked by the durchstich in 20. District. We where very close to where Ron and rob lived, Uncle Rudy had remarried, he had an apartment, close to us and the big boys where skiing. I and rob had a sleight. Winter was beautiful then; aunty Peppy was staying with us and took care of us. She loved Otto most and she gave him a pet name, schnoten. By night she would dream of Otto and would call his name first in a low tone and she would go louder and louder, until she woke the whole family up. She called Rosy by her real name, but me, she called Meissen porcelain, that was a very fragile China, but if I made her angry, she would call me yellow canary.

Mamma was in hospital, giving birth, to our youngest brother. Daddy was having a very bad mood and as usual he would beat Otto, Aunty peppy went to help Otto and Papa hit her on the eye that Auntie's eye swell shut. Even then, I hated our father, when he got so violent. But then I did not know why he did this. Poor Aunty peppy had to move in, with our Grandmother, she was the only one who went with our mother true thin and thick, Aunty hated her Sister and had to live with her, not to long and aunty Peppy was placed in a home, by her Sister. When Mamma gets home, they had another fight, about what Daddy did, to our Aunty and Otto. Mamma was livid. But she could not get Aunty back with our Dad. My little brother came home and there was no more Aunties, Rosy and Otto, had to go school in the day and perform with Dad, in the evening.Mamma was presumably by her girlfriend aunty Mel and I had to stay home, watching my new brother Billy. We had a very cold winter that year; in 1955. As soon as spring arrived we went on tour again. We also had a small carnival next to the high wire and we went to perform in Home Wand Aria, one day in Felbring we had a very distinguish guest, my Mothers Brother and his family, this was the first time I met them. we where surprised he came and was not ashamed for us ,after all he was Major and a big Politician in Land Tag , but he told one and all this is my little sister and her family. He was living in a big villa with a maid and a cook and had 5 children. Witch he adored. He brought gifts for us and he gave Mamma 2000 Schilling, she said no Adi and he said this is the least I can do for my Sister. I always wondered why we had not parents like that who loved us and cared for us. Our parents treated us like animals, where treated in the circus, just perform and make money and all we get is a pat on the head, but more often then not, poor Otto always get licks, somehow he always got of the wrong side, of our father. This summer, I see some Boys, who wanted to kill some chicks and I ask them to give me the chicks. They said they are falcons and would grow up to kill chicks, I said no matter I want them and paid them 20 Schilling, for the chicks. So I raised the falcons and feed them raw liver and they grow big, they would sit on my shoulder and where completely tame, one day I come home from school, there was no falcons, Mother ordered them killed, by our workers. That was when a real rift developed between us. I could not believe she did this to me. Mother was not much better, than Daddy, she never mended our close for us; she never bought close for us. Instead she takes us, to Red Cross to beg clothing for us. Daddy had his costumes and beside that he had no dissent clothing, but Mamma had a very heavy winter coat with fur lining, gold jewelry and elegant clothing. She never cooks breakfast for us and lay in bed, till Daddy serves her breakfast, in bed. Every day she complained, the coffee tastes like sleeping feet, to cold, the coffee is to hot, the buns are too old. So she protested every day and our father said nothing to her, but watch out, if he drink something, she just shut up and says nothing, she would just blend in to the background and Otto had to go immediately to bed, so Papa cant see him , or Otto would get it again. Until I was nine, Mamma would cook at noon and make a coffee and bread for supper. Papa's brother Rudy was the only one, of his brothers, who regular visit us. He supported us children, Mamma and Papa did not want him, to give us money, but when ever he came, he would shake my hand and but ten schilling in my hand, so no one knows. That way I always go to the movies. As I was eight years old, Otto was 14 years old and he took care, of the business. He wanted a new, more modern, performance for us, so he put a new act together, with a motorcycle and a trapeze. We would span, our steel wire to the church towers and have on the other side a short mast, about 6 meter high and behind the mast a big tractor, where the wire was tied to, also in front of the tractor we had two meter Anker to secure the wire. We also had a Java 350 to ride on the wire under the Java was a trapeze and Daddy and Otto would take turns ride the motorcycle. Mamma and I was on the trapeze. Also I sat on Otto's shoulders when he was riding the motorcycle, up on the wire.this winter; our parents had the brilliant idea to perform in winter with a travelling theater.

That winter was so cold, it was horrible. Our parents, where sleeping in the big trailer and we had to sleep in a small trailer, with very thin aluminum walls, plus no heating. Again I had to go to a new school, every second day. I had to perform a comic sketch, with my Daddy, I was playing a stupid thirty boy, who had to go to Sunday school, Daddy was the teacher, he was a Tiger on the high wire, but performing was not his strength. He always forget his lines and I would touch him with my foot under the table and whisper his lines to him.Rosy was also not happy performing she had to play the love interest to our brother Otto and he did not like it either.the stuffed a pillow in his back and made him appear a hunchback and he had to wear a mustache like Hitler and they had to kiss all the wile ,they where so embarrassed. Rosy also had to perform as a fast painter and draw pictures in two minutes. Billy was also performing , they call that ingarisch , He was doing tricks on or Fathers hands ,it went quite well and we made a lot of money, in summer we where working with the motor sickle again and we had our carnival.one day I was watching the boat swing and there was a very strong boy in the swing, he swing so wild , that the board, where you stop the little boat (swing)fell to the side and the boat keel hit me full blast over the head ,I was bathed in blood and rosy had to carry me to the hospital ,riding the public Bus I received a tonsure (shave of the head like the monks)and four stitches and an x-ray. Mother was not worried at all about me.

Mother never saved any money, they would by a new rigen or a tractor but they never bought a house, mostly she spends the money Willy nilly. all the time they had people hanging with us and taking advantage of us ,they had a guy working for us who had open tuberculosis and mother said no matter we are all vaccinated by birth for that ,but I was disgusted of him and I insist I have my own cub, plates and cutlery. we had Lillian porcelain and the settings came in different colors my own was light blue and one day I found out he used my plates and cup just to spite me ,so I drew it in the rubbish pin and told my mother to by me a new one and I said anytime he uses it I will throw it away again. he had a face cream and toiletries like a woman and I throw all away to ,so in the morning he could not find his toiletries and ask anyone where it was ,nobody knows. Mamma was expecting a baby again and in November we took winter quarters in Inzersdorf next to Vienna I Always looked at the skyline and yarned to go back to Vienna.I hated school there ,the children where very nasty.mamma send me out to sell paper flours so she could get cigarettes, alto she was in her 7th month she still smocked.

Billy was dressed like an American, he was almost three Years old and he had long blond locks and big brown eyes anywhere you go with him people said how cute he was. he always had a pacifier in his mouth like a pipe and he could talk like he is big boy, he had an American toy Jeep and if it mashed up he need a new one. Mamma send Rosy to grandma to pick up a package from America for us , aunty Heed said it was there.Rosy went with her Red Coat and cap it was very cold that Day. rosy came back with out a coat just her red cap and shawl she was bluish so cold it was.turns out aunty rose ,mammas sister was by Grandma ,when Rosy get there she took of her Coat and said she comes to pick up our packages.they said 'we got no baggage ' so rosy said ; I know they are there and mamma send me for them 'aunt rose slapped her on both sides of her face take her by her shoulders and throw rosy out the door with no Coat. So Rosy had to go across Vienna with the tram wearing no coat, in December people looked at rosy as if she was crazy. Mamma went ballistic and gone to Klosterneuburg where aunt rose had her house, she met her brother in law by the garden door and he would not let her in.; He said your sister is not home'. so mamma said ' is fine by me and You get the licks ' mamma really beat him up good and went home ,very angry at all of them.Grandma had put her Sister Aunty Peppy in a home for the elderly and when she got mortally ill , she was placed I a hospital.Mamma went there and she took Billy along.Aunty Peppy was always happy to see Mamma she was to her like a daughter and Mamma really loved her to. At Christmas Day, our Aunty Peppy Died and her last Dying wish was a little bit of Tyrolean earth on her grave. Not even little whish was granted to her. She dedicated her whole life to our Grand mother and our Mother and She was awarded wit nothing but abuse. It was very sad. The children in school called me a gipsy, as I sit in my bench reading. when we had the break some of them squeeze me between Desk and chair , somehow I get out of it just before the teacher got back in and I told her ,but to no avail ,so at the next break ,the leader try to pass by my desk and I stretched out my leg and trip him ,he was sliding all the way to the front row ! and then all of them gang up on me, but I fought with the whole class, I took the chair and just hit anyone, I could get, with it ,there was an uproar, but I was much better than them ,I won against the whole class , me the gipsy . when the Teacher came, She wanted to admonish me in front of the class, but I took my schoolbag and went home.the same day, I was expelled from school I did not care I was happy about that.after this, we moved back to Vienna Schlosshoferstrasse 21 district, where the oldest brother of Anton, had a piece of land, fenced in with a wooden plank. My Sister was borne there, on the 7th of January 1958. Otto said' if she ever has a baby again, I will leave immediately ,I am sick and tired of this " Melanie was healthy , but mamma had badly inflamed breast and could not nurse her so they had to by a baby formula for her ,so papa was working in a factory ,to feed us.in the 11th of January 1958 I had my 9th birthday, mamma turned 35 in the 10th January 1958 and of Corse there where no gifts Rosy turn 18 on the January 21st 1958.we where ashamed the youngest and the oldest where 18 years apart. It was bitter cold, Otto had no winter gloves, his hands where red from the frost where he had to carry his heavy school bag, so I gave him one of my gloves, so we both had one hand in the pocket and with the gloved hand we carried our school bag. in addition I had no winter coat Just a jacked, witch was cut so bad I looked like the hunchback of Notre dame in it.and the boots I had on where indescribable. I Always had to go shop for uncle Fred who was 83 years old and had asthma ,but he still smoked aqua filter cigarettes.one day in January I go to get his cigarettes ,as I came back , he want me to see his book ,I take a look and was shocked ,it was a very large book with all sorts of naked people in it in all different positions ,as soon as I realize watt's going on I want to bolt , but he stepped in my way and said ' look what I got here and pull out a very large penis ,I was going to pass out in fear ,I blanched and he said ; come touch it ,its for you "I just run toward him and squeeze out beside him and bolt out of the door like a filly ,out of the stables.after that, I made shore he don't see me again.'My mamma said aren't you go shopping for Uncle Fred again? No, I said definitely not, I got no time and he never pays me "and that was that, I never allow myself again to be alone with a man, other than my father or brother.

Not long after that they had a tiff with Fred and moved to another location in the same district and we could remain, in our school.all of a sudden they had a new friend , a Serbo-Croatian artist who had two Sons and a Daughter ,she was married to a Circus Artist and was somewhere on tour, with her husbands troupe ,the had a large group, forming human pyramids as high, as fife persons high , the top person ,was always a small child, the had a trampoline and from there they would salto on to the pyramid, a very dangerous act ,one of them already broke his neck ,the same man, Donner was a trainer and trained his own Sons to. for instance Rudy his oldest son , had to learn saltos and one day he stood on a table and had to salto down from there ,Rudy did not but his body, in the correct manner , Donner hit Rudy in midair ,so bad ,that Rudy trooped to the ground , like a lame duck ,his second Son had to learn glitshnick ,that is a contortionist ,the same thing, what I did playfully and he received lots of beatings ,I always said Donner is a cruel pervert. I was playfully doing tricks ,like cross both my legs behind my head and walk like this on my hands ,just now I found out that is also done in yoga ,I must have that in my genes, from the Indians.I also loved to dance and my brother and I where dancing acrobatic rock and roll when where very good at it and Otto had all the singles from Elvis Presley ,Jerry Lee Luis ,Great balls of Fire ,Fats Domino ,Jack Berry ,we also had the music from the Guy who wore the hair rollers and the head tie ,little Richard , he was great fun ,my favorite was good golly miss molly and also hit the road jack and don't you come back no Moore no Moore, from the blind singer ,Ray Charles , we had them all must have been a hundred of them. Otto show me how to jump on him and feel still light and we where real good we had every trick in the book, I jumped like a flee on him and bend back to the ground going into a hand stand and he take my hands and I slide true his legs and twist onto his back again, it was the thing we enjoyed most. my parents always had friends over and the entertainment was that everybody had to perform something ,Rudy was a great trumpet player and he always played for us ,I was a good dancer and I performed a belly dance for them ,alto I had no belly. I was the sugar doll from the belly dance troupe, it was great fun. but then my mother and Donner did some brain storming and said I was very talented and must become an extortionist we call it kautjuck ,and that means rubber.Herr Donner started to train me and he immediately hurt me a lot.he would start with 'weichmachen' that is a form of stretching ,I had to stand facing him ,my face on his belly ,so short I was and put my arms around his middle ,he would take first one of my calves and then the other ,and bring them towards his shoulders, he was supposed to precede slowly ,but apparently he loved to hurt people and did it in one swift motion and was not satisfied to but my feet on his chest no he , put my feet on his shoulder blade ,so my back was bent like a very small U and he let me stay like this for fife minutes after that he put me with my back to the wall and squeezed me with his whole body weight against the wall one of his fat legs firmly planted against one of my legs then he took the other leg and lift it up to my shoulder ,to stretch it for the split ,I can still remember the pain of that.this always tock place one hr before breakfast. I had to make 20 bridges 20 splits and 20 handstands, after 1 hour I got breakfast and then I went school. After school the same and then lunch ,homework , and at fife o clock another hr training ,a cup of coffee one bread and butter ,no fruits ,no vitamins.after six weeks in February Donner became real angry at me and said to my mother ' frau schebl 'he could not say our name right the name is Schobel 'Frau schebl she is resisting me she dos not want to do it ,she is very nimble but I cant work with her ,she only need another two centimeters to make a spagat '.I now something was coming and I had had it ,I run away out in the snow in my leotard and my little leather slippers ,it took Otto about 5 minutes to catch me.he carried me back and then it got serious , when I made the spagat again, Donner pushed me down on my shoulders and Otto had to sit one of my legs and Rudy on the other ,they left me so for twenty minutes.after that I was able to do the split . I was so angry that I hated all of them.every waking minute, I wonder what to do ,even Otto helped them it was unbelievable.the next morning I see him coming ,he had a real square head like a box and gray hear on the side of his head and bushels of gray hear coming out his nose and his ears ,his teeth where square like his head , he also had stubby fingers and a very cynical manner ,I Just could have killed him ,if I could ,a real old bastard. He said' nundy kreize einbegen!' that means back bending 'I said Herr Donner zunge in mein arsch einbiegen!'That means bend your tongue in my ass! 'Frau Schebel You hear what she said "she heard and she took the plastic rug beater and beat me so I had black weals all over my body! after this it get worse I could do longer go to exercise class in school because I was covered in welts and child services would have taken me away from my parents and put me in a home, if they found out Austria has strict laws in that and then you stay there till you 21 Years old, I preferred the beating. In April we moved to Inzersdorf by Wien, to get ready for the season. the Trainer had me learn Moore tricks, so I had to go from handstand to bridge and then in to the split and vice versa, I passed out a lot and when I wake up they laving at me and said look how Yellow she is in her face look the ugly bitch, there and then I realize that my family is a bunch of maniacs. No normal people at all. Melanie was four months old when my parents send Rosy to America, at this time rosy was the mother for Billy and Melanie, but they send her so she could make a way for us to get there. she was performing with mammas family.I had now two children to look after ,and had so much training that I walked like a automat with cherky motions ,I could hardly lift my legs ,people on the road would say to me ',do you need help ?' I said 'no thank you I am allride'then finally the trainers Younger son came to visit.he was always playing soccer with my brother and started to have one shoulder up and one down very awkward and all of a sudden he had a Big hunchback ,his father had crippled him ,I realize ,so when Donner left I said to my mum' and now you got to kill me ,because I am not willing to do this again. and that was the end of it.surprisingly my mother left me alone, but to the end of her life she was angry that I resisted her, and I was angry that she put me true this hell, especially when I developed a series back pain, once I was paralyzed for four weeks and had to crawl on the floor to go to the Bathroom, my hips are giving me big problems to ,just as I am writing this words I am in agony again I cant even stand 5 minutes and all the hate comes back to me as if it was yesterday. I know all this has to do with perverted Donner. we went on tour the first time without rosy and we missed her ,Otto was 15 and looked like 20 his friends called him Elvis.he wore leather jacked and leather pants and would ride a small motorcycle and of cores the big motorcycle on the high wire.we got two new helpers this summer ,they where refugees from east Germany Ursula was from Pommern and Hermann was from east Berlin ,together they escaped from the Russians and where homeless on the road sins they fled ,the strictly lived from begging and occasional a little Job and slept in Hey Barns. I was very sorry for them Ursula always cried and said I will never see home again.I don't know what's happening to my family. Ursula was supposed to cook for us while mamma went with Otto location haunting.one day she said to me 'I am in deep trouble now, your mother said to cook marillenknoedel ! (Sweet fruit dumplings) what I am going to do? I am afraid she will fire me! Help Me.' I always observed my mother cooking and remember how to make the dumplings and I cook them real good! Ursula was amazed! She said to me 'do elender nachtwaechter do "this is a jock and means I am a bad night watch man." My Mother never no, that I cooked the food. Otto was very unhappy to share his trailer with them, because he had no privacy. Hermann always made fun of the farmers and ask them if they need a helper who eat your speck and eggs and fornicate with your wife he was a real character.One day a German tourist said to him (you mutilate the environment with Your placards! Hermann said (Schnauze ,Luftschnapper elendiger ,oder ich Knall dir eine form latz dass dier samtliche gesichts zuege entgleisen)that means, shut up ,air breather or I bust your face that you loose all your facial impressions. One morning Ursel und Hermann where gone they could not stand to be with my Brother to, we guessed.

Image 5# Otto Nundy Meli and Billy 1959 goes here !

Aldo the war was long gone there where still a lot of people who where Nazis ,they always think that they have a right to treat us like trash, but they want to watch us, perform, free and call us Gipsy and beat on us, many times I was selling tickets, people try to cuss me ,but my brother had like an antenna for that always his fist would appear like magic ,and they assailants would Just fly true the air ,get on there feet and run.Otto was very strong.one day this summer our Tractor was not working ,so our Father, hired a man with a tractor, to move us from one town to the next ,there was the tractor pulling our trailer and behind the trailer, they hitched the trailer, with the mast and the Anker ,as well as the motor sickle and the trapeze on it together, this was about 20 meters long. Daddy sat next to the driver on the tractor ,Otto , Mamma ,Me and little Billy where behind in the trailer.the road was very curvy going to very wooded , for alps, as we where overtaken, in the Curve by two busses ,one with women and one with men ,the sharply stopped in front of us and all the men came out of the Bus. The driver first ,he was the gang leader, apparently the where all drunk and screamed how we ruined the Bus ,a group of about ten men ,went for my Dad and pull him off the tractor, no one even bother with the driver, the must have known, He is a farmer like them, so he could not be blamed. Mamma went for a big Iron Anker, swinging it over her head and said "but my Husband down you Idiots, or I smash your Heads." The but Daddy down very carefully and Otto, hit the Driver, on his eye and they eye closed instant and swell big like a orange, all of them, the entire Bus, went for Otto, He run and jumped in the trailer, one of the double doors, was locked ,so only one Person, at the time could pass. The Driver on His heel, Otto crabbed the metal soup scoop, from the rack above the kitchen stove, the driver by the door said, "you little Boy. " Yes Otto said, but the little boy closed your Eye and if you don't drive off, together with your gang, I will close your other eye to and who will drive you all, when you blind? But if you like, one after the other can pass true this Door and I will knock you, all to the ground." As fast as they came at us, just as fast they left, wit out another word. I, as a little girl, could not believe the cowardnes and wickedness of this act. There was only one conclusion, stay away from privet people; they would kill us if they could, for no reason at all. Billy was four years old and I became more protective to him, he always came in troubles, he had long blond locks, he wanted no hair cut and big brown eyes, with very thick dark eyelashes and he had a pacifier, shaped like a heart, in his mouth, taking it out, only when he eat, he really looked like a girl. Children would say, 'o what a pretty girl 'to him, he did not like that and would stamp his foot and say "no I am not a Girl!" "Don't lie I can see you are a Girl!" O Yea, you want to see it? Look here' and he pull down his shorts and say," now you see, I am a Boy! Otto was already repairing all our vehicles, he learned that from our Father and Billy would, stand next to him, when he was working and asked questions, he also know, every Car type, just ask Billy and he tell you what a car this is. He was also performing with us, Melanie was too small. We got no word from Rosy, she was lost to us, or so it seemed I was wondering, why she did not come back home. Otto and I, where always close, but we came closer, sins Rosy left. We only had each other, when Otto was 16 Years old, He was looking like he was twenty and the woman where crazy for him ,one day two German Tourists asked Me, who the Guy is, with the chocolate eyes, I know ,they where in heat. I said "that's my Brother "'how old is he?"Ask him, I said, He can talk "well they asked him all ride, after the performance, He did not come home all night. He had sex with the two of them and came back, at nine o clock in the morning, our mother was livid, but Otto was Happy. The next winter we where not in Vienna. Instead we where in Neunkirchen and my mother, had one of our Cousins, next to us with her trailer. She was married to a puppet player and they would perform in schools. They made me watch, there two Girls, but the Girls, where just Crying when they left, nonetheless I had to watch them. On top of that Mother had this couple staying with us; he was a Musician and had Yellow skin from catching malaria, in world war two. She was supposed to cook for us, but the food was lousy. Otto had to go to work in a factory and drive there in the bitter cold, with his motor sickle and almost freeze his Noose and Ears off, so Mamma could have her servants.

One Day the women sit Billy on the table, witch was next to the Oven ,so she could wash the floor, Billy fell down with His upper arm, against the oven and got badly burned. Of Corse I got the blame for it. I don't' know why, but I get the licks anyway. The next time she cooks a big pot of Soup and had it, not in the middle of the oven, but on the edge of the oven. Melanie was Just a Year old and had her left hand on the handle of the oven and was stretching her right Hand, standing on her tip toes, like a ballerina, to crab the handle of the Soup Pot. I get her just in time, or Melanie would have been dead. Those are the kind of idiotic, people my parents had around us, I was really angry. Otto got Sick and I the next day, we where resting in the bunk beds and Missis Val, sat outside, on the Sofa knitting. I know she was there, so I started a conversation with Otto. Loud enough for her to hear. I said ,'I wonder how long they going to keep this idiots, they almost kill Melanie and Billy, that ugly old bitch, with her strudel legs, she cant even eat, always an open mouth, that her food falls out. I also tired of eating her nasty food. Yea, Otto said I agree and I have to give Mamma, all my money to feed them. She Jumped up and said, „I Am Going to tell your Mother, You bastards.'She said, we where laughing and she slammed the Door. Good riddance we said and the next day, by dawn they where gone they where afraid of us, Otto was a grown man and they said nothing, to our Mother. This summer Otto teaches me, to drive his HMW off-road motor sickle and it was fun riding it I felt very important being able to drive. Otto loved to go fishing and he made a sling with a plastic line and but on his goggles, on the plastic line, he had a piece of bread , He but His head in the water and when the fish bit the bread, Otto closed the noose and give me the fish, to kill. I don't know, where I took the guts to do it, but I always did what he said. And with time, I became more a boy, than a girl. The next Season, Otto took our cousin Ron, with us on tour and we did everything alone our Dad was semi retired. He did not like that at all. Almost every evening, Daddy had some drinks, before performances and he was like a time bomb, waiting to go off, and the next two Years Otto would run away often. Otto was going to driving school and as soon as he was 18 Years old, he collected his Drivers permit and from then on, we Just went to far away places, like to Maria Taferl and Oberoesterreich where all the big Churches are and to Steiermark and we made a better business, than ever this Year. As we where in Oberoesterreich a telegram came, that my mothers Father, had died of stomach cancer. They left me alone with the children and went to the funeral, to Vienna. I was twelve Years old. In autumn 1961 we finally heard of Rosy.

At the same time, Rosy was not happy in America, she had to call them Mamma and Papa, so nobody knows that she was an illegal alien, the made no papers for her and she was a slave worker, with no pay, not even a cent.

Rosy had to bathe the twins, the twins where very good, trapeze artist then and where only 5 years old, they where the stars, of the show and Rosy was the mother. Rosy also had to cook and clean, perform two times a day and get no health insurances. One day, she fell of the wire and broke her other ankle and get no medical attention at all. They where even bigger animals then our parents! Not even one letter she could send, in four years. They had her passport and she could go nowhere. Rosy had a good friend in Florida, her name was Gladys. But I don't understand why Gladys did not help rosy to contact us? The Years went on, Rosy was for years in the states and was not allowed a boyfriend and get no money paid. When they had an interview at the Andy Williams show and performed in Madison Square Garden, Rosy met some of Anton's relatives in New York. Mamma's youngest half brother and her half sister were also in the states. Kristy was married to one of Anton's nephew and they had a very good act on the Circus, Kristy was very beautiful, green eyes and reed hair and a figure to die for. They had a long ladder where he walked up on and balanced Kristy, standing on his head, on one foot. She had a feadher head dress and long gloves, plus a sparkly leotard with feathers on her hips. She looked unbelievable beautiful. They also made head on head, head stands. They always had very much better costumes than the Anton's, Kristi was also making there own costumes and they performed at all the big circus shows, also with the tree stooges. Willy her brother was not very talented but he had grandmother's good looks brown eyes and brown hair, widow's peak broad shoulders and slim body, he looked like a young Gregory Peck and he was a lady's man. Anton did not like Willis his new girlfriend, because he was also a helper in His troupe and he, forbade Willy to see her again. So Willy runs away with her to New York. He worked there as a construction worker on one of they high buildings when he fell off the 3rd floor, he had so many broken bones and some of his brain matter coming out, he was delirious and Anton had him moved to Tampa hospital so his Sister Henni and he could look after him. In the beginning, it did not look like he will survive, he was delirious and Anton, had to be there, at hand to hold him down, he was very strong, and had to be restrained most of the time. After about six weeks and several surgeries, he woke up and was put in a body cast and they had him at home at this time, most of the time when he was alone with his nice that is Kristie's daughter, she was nine years old, she was very bad to him and left him on the bedpan for hrs on end and she did what she could to make his live misery. It took a year, of physic therapy, to be able to walk, with a heavy limp and a Kane. What goes around comes around, he got paid, for his badness with my Mother, she was in prison one year and he was very ill, for one year. They say Rosy had sex, with Anton and when Aunt Henni catch them, Rosy run away, with very little money and no Passport, she made it, to another relative, in Brooklyn New York, who had a donate shop. She met Portorican and still sends no letter home. Mammas sister Kristy had a house in New Jersey and she finally alarmed my Mother about what's going on, Kristy's, husband was telling Anton, to send Rosés Passport to them, or he would go to the Immigration Services. So Anton had no choice as to send the passport. We performed until November to send the money, for Rosy to come home again.

Chapter 3

OTTINIS jun., weltbester Schrägseil-
künstler vor dem gefahrvollen Auftritt

3. Chapter
November 1961 Rosy Comes Back!

Finally, Rosy arrived on a very cold November day. She had very pretty clothes on, all gifts from Aunty Kristy, a nice hair style, the pony tail was gone and she looked like a lady. She had four pieces of luggage, one of them for me. I was very happy, to get my big sister back and when she opened that luggage, I could not believe, the pretty things she bring for me, a red silk Cocktail gown and coat, a very pretty umbrella and hand bag, things I never dreamed of getting, it was like Christmas, she would make sandwiches for us and spoiled everyone rotten, like a real Mother. Rosy got very ill, probably because she missed her boyfriend, for a while it looked, like she lost it. She hoped that my parents, would send for Him, but I know this would not happened. Rosy was changed; she was a new person, all together. She even brought new customs for us. That Christmas was nice, a new beginning. As soon as spring came around, we started to practice and Otto was surprised, that I could walk on the high wire alone. Because, I never did that before, I only walked with my daddy, and sins I was eight years old, I was just on Otto's shoulders, or on the trapeze. When we left for the season, we really stepped up work Otto had made new masts and if there was no church tower, we used our masts. They were no longer of wood, but of metal and Otto, designed and welded them himself. We children had an aluminum trailer where we slept and the big Circus Trailer was for our parents. We moved in the morning, to the next town, put up the rigen in the afternoon and performed at night, every day, a different school in June. I stopped going to school. Because the where not in town, anymore when school was over and they had to come back for me to pick me up. I hated that. Cousin Ron was with us again and Otto and he where sleeping in Otto's mini bus, so they could have sex with the girls every night and there was plenty of them. I still wonder, if there is a child of my brother, somewhere out there. Rosy and I went swimming in Amstetten and Rosy was driving the mofa, with me on the back seat. Going there was ok, because it was downhill ,but coming back, proved to be difficult, the hill was very steep and rosy had about 80 kg together, with my 46 kilo that was to much, so the motor started sputtering and I, just but my feet on the ground and stood, Rosy still driving in slow motion, the HMW went bwwwwwuiup and the motor died, Rosy let her self, ever so slowly fall to the left and burned her leg badly, on the muffler and was vexed with me ,but what could I have don? When we had a long distance, we put the trailers and tractor on the train and followed with the VW Bus, most the time Mamma and Otto went ahead of us, location hunting and advertising. Our troupe was very big, Rosy Otto, Ron, me, Billy, Melly and Daddy. Daddy did not like, that he was not the main man, again and started to fight with Mamma again and again, one day he said,' I am leaving you, I will get a divorce and never come back, the next day He was back.

Nobody took him seriously anyway. Rosy, had a very good microphone voice and made the announcements In English and German. Otto, one day out of the blue, said he will make the Headstand, while he drive up on the wire. It was very difficult. He practiced and practiced, he made the headstand, on the headlight of the motor sickle and had his tip toes on the saddle and slowly spread his legs like a fork and drives off in a head stand legs like a fork. He missed at least fifty times, but he did not give up, until he found the right speed and he just licked this puppy. The next thing was me. I had to sit on His shoulders and when we reached the top of the wire, I had to stand up on Otto's shoulders. It was very difficult to balance, because the motor sickle that Otto sat on and me standing up, on His shoulders, was longer, than the trapeze below, plus the wind, up there was very high and so, I would start to sway on top, I had to do every movement, in slow motion and it seemed an eternity, to steady myself. We started to perform the new tricks in Linz. It was 13 stories high and we had the press coming there. It was a resounding success. At times we where like twenty stories up, but this did not satisfy Otto. We worked our way true Oberoesterreich, to Salzkammergut and there we performed in very posh places. In one of them, Rosy did one of her stunts, every town we get, they had at least one Idiot and as usual, they had the heat, for Rosy and followed her all over the place, this time Rosy got angry, but the guy, would not leave her alone, so She asked Him,' what is Your name?" My name is Gottlieb!" He said and I want to fuck you!'" O Yea she goes and do you have a place for that?"" Yes He said, in the church."" Aha' Rosy goes and probably you got a small Dick!"'"No, no, my Dick is so long!"And He made a Fist and indicated with his left hand, that his Dick is as long as half His underarm, Rosy and I started laughing and said," we don't belief you", he said he will show us, 'Rosy said' go behind the Trailer and I look out the window and see. '. We went in the Trailer and looked out the Window. He was already there opened his fly and took out his Dick. His dick was for real, as big as he said. I almost died in shock, but Rosy did not miss a beat, when he said;' can I fuck you now?'"First I need a big chocolate cake from the Konditorei and make shore it is packet up good, so I get real horny."We where confident, not to see him again, but In about twenty minutes , he came back with a pink box from the Konditorei and in it, was the best looking chocolate torte, I have ever seen. That's when Otto came back and admonished Rosy, what She is doing, with the Idiot and then he told the Idiot, what he want from his wife and sister, "he said and don't came back here, or I call the police and they throw you in Jail, that helped and we did not see him again. Our brother got very angry, with Rosy and warned her, never to do something like that again.

Otto also stretched the wire, across the water and on to the church tower, in Altmuenster on Gmundener See and the distance was extremely long and high; on top of that, the water is like a magnet, pulling you down. It was absolutely, exhilarating to work like this; we liked it, when the audience was in fear for our lives. Also the bigger the audience was, the better we performed. It was rewarding.

In Gmunden, there was a very beautiful girl, she was a model, Rosy catch Otto talking to her and said to her," what do you want from my Husband! You home wrecker, we got two children, right over there!"She indicated Melly and Billy to her. Lucky for Otto, he could clear that up and after we left, he had, a long distance, relation ship with dad girl he was really taken by her. From then He always watched for Rosy. One day in Villach we stretched the wire across the river again and there was a very strong current. Otto and Ron almost broke there backs , when the wire got moist , from the rain before and the brakes where not responding, Otto and Ron, slid back the wire and got discharged from the trapeze and the motorcycle, flying true the air, lucky nothing serious happened to them, they could have been death. Another day the whole rigen collapsed and I gained consciousness, sticking with my face in the sand heap that saved my live. Every day, they mobbed us for autographs, hoping to get sex too, including poor me. Well Otto had none of this, he would say, 'sorry the young lady, is not giving any autographs today „and to me 'in the trailer and don't come out again till morning!' after this his job was done and he and Ron would get the girls. Rosy never had a date and was like Cinderella waiting for the prince.We where in salzkammergut that is where all the tourists go, very beautiful lake's surrounded by mountains, after putting up the riggen, we went swimming every day! In Villach near the Italian border Rosy took me to the hairdresser and had my hair, bleached blond, so I looked like Brigit Bardot. That drove the boys crazy. Millstadt am Milstaettersee was especial beautiful and our mother said, that her Mother was born there, when our great great, parents where touring, with the theater. The water was a turquoise color and we swam out far to a water-ski ramp and stayed there, at least two hours. It was so far out; our Mother could not see us! When we came back, Mother was walking up and down the beach, with her straw hat, hands on her back, like aunty peppy would have done and said 'where where you all so long! I dough you all drowned!' I said 'what kind of a Mother are you? You should have called rescue to save us, instead you wait for us to drown?' She was so relived, that she did nut cuss me out. Soon after this we performed in St.Wolfgang am Wolfgangsee that is where the famous operetta plays and they also made a movie there? Otto tock me up to the church, to strap the wire up and he had to test me, if I am scared in the dark, he always did that! We had a big success in St, Wolfgang. There where so many people, you could walk on the heads. I alone cashed six thousand schilling and all of us where selling tickets, Rosy must have cashed twenty thousand shilling. That year alone we could have bought a house, but Mother was a very bad banker, nobody knows, what she did with the money. Rosy had a date and we where watching her, as she sit down by the café and ordered two drinks and nobody came. Mamma and Otto made fun of her, I think they where very cruel. Poor rosy was heart sick. She was 22 years old and never had a date, sins she came back to Austria. She had to wash, cook and look after Melly and Billy. In the day time, I run behind them, but before performance, she had to get them ready, not that they did something important, they where just window dressing. Rosy took it all in strive, but one day she really got mad, Mamma said," go and wash the children and make it snappy! 'Rosy said, 'go and wash this whoring bastards yourself. 'Well that was it, Rosy had to pack her suit case and Otto had to put her, on the next train to Vienna. Grandma was glad to take her, for she had, a free maid in the house, Rosy went to work in Wiener Prater that is a big landmark and amusement park. We kept on working, like nothing happened, there was Otto and Ron two very handsome, Young Men and Billy Melly and last but not least me. Everybody just wanted to see, Otto and me. As our tour was winding down, we made our way back to Vienna and performed in Bruck a der Mur. The church tower was so high, that the wind almost blow me off, that was the only time, I was really scared. I am glad; I don't have to go back there. In October, we came back to Vienna, to our winter quarters, next to our sinti cousins. I went back to my old school and Otto found a Job as a Truck driver, he would pick up Oranges from Sparta. That is in Greece and brings them to Vienna, always when he came home, he would bring a big box of oranges for us. Rosy took a Job working in a hair supply, when the Wiener Prater closed for the winter. She was four months pregnant, she did not say, who the Baby Daddy was. I could not believe, she was really happy, about it and she would say, " look, Nundy, I got mother hands now,'I said, but they look the same as always.' Mother reconciled with Rosy, now that she could get money from her, every week and Otto had to give her money to, so that was nice for Mammy , above all she loved Money! I went to school and every time, Uncle Rudi came to visit, he would give me money, so I can go to the Poppenwimmer Kino. I watched Hatari and all this nice movies with Audrey Hepburn and Grace Kelly, Liz Taylor, Gina Lolo Brigida, Brigitte Bardot and I dreamed about, being just as beautiful and Rich and live in a Posh Villa, After this I go back to sleep in my cold trailer. If I could not go to the Kino, I would read a book, I loved reading, this was always a way, to escape the misery, for me. In January we had lots of snow and Otto was already one week late to come back. The snow was very deep, to the knees, I was home alone as usual, when I heard, a car horn blow, I now my brother had returned and I was happy, but I did not go out, because it was so cold, all of a sudden, I hear a scratching on the door, I was thinking, he is playing one of his pranks again, with me and as I open the door, Otto is lying in the snow, by the door,' he said I cannot walk, my back is hurting me, why did you not come, when I blow the horn? 'Otto had 90 kg and no help, near anywhere, I just make him, put his arms about my neck and I Put my arms about Him and schlepped him to the bed. I was so scared for him, up to this day, I don't' know how I did that, I was strong, from the trapeze work, but still, I must have had maybe 48 Kilo the most. I undressed him and start up the fire, made him tea and bread with butter and gave him a hot water bottle on his back. He said he was snowed in, in the Yugoslavian mountains for about 5 days. He had to wait till they cleared the road. That time he was lucky, there was a little wooden house, from a sheep herder and there was an oven, otherwise he would freeze to death there. Otto could not leave the bed, for about four weeks, all the time, He was alone with me, and our mother was not there. I was looking after him , in the morning he would say, ' please can I get my coffee, ''jess I said only if you say cra, cra, cra and flap your wings like a nice Crow, then You get it. Our Grandmother said he was a Crow, because of His black hair, we always play these childish pranks, but what else could we do? In these four weeks, we discussed our future and Otto said I should learn good and he will pay for me, to go to fashion school and when I finish that, we go to America. It looked like things, where looking up and there was hope, we would get away soon. The Postman came and he brought a letter for Otto, he must have been expecting something and' he said what is it?'I said 'a letter from your Girlfriend! "Bring it to me 'no I said if you don't' come for it, I will read it to you! Otto stood up strait and came for the letter! He was walking again. In March Mammas Sister Kristy and Her Family Came to Vienna, they had a Motorcycle act, not by far as good as ours and the where performing, in the Stadthalle in Vienna, the year was 1963 and the Austrians where still poor, but they came with there pink Caddy lack from New York via Hamburg on a big boat. Mamma went to visit and Otto to, Otto wanted to go to America, with them, but they did not want Otto, he was too good and instead they took our cousin Ron who could definitely do nothing. We where surprised, that Ron left Austria, just like that. His father had a nasty divorce earlier and the step mother put Ron and Rob, into a home for bad children. Ron got out but Rob had to stay there he was only going to be thirteen and had to stay for another four Years or so. Rob was abused there they made Him stand naked on the cold tiles and throw water at him. When he told his father abbot it, Uncle Rudy made a scandal and they throw him out. So poor Rob was totally alone most of the time. Now that His brother went to America, he got nobody again. I felt that Ron was a traitor. They took Him to America anyhow. As soon as the whether was warm, we started practicing, full throttle on the wire, Otto took another of our cousins, as a partner, he needed a second Man and he would stand on Peters , shoulders and jump down on the wire without a balancing stick, he also would jump over me and and jump rope, all on the wire. This was going to be our, new number for America! He also had a roll and a board and he stand on the board, with me on his shoulders and balanced like that, he said we will not wait any longer we go in July to America, nobody was more happy than I. Otto was already saving money, for the tickets for us Otto, Peter and I, we joust went near Vienna to perform and Otto had his new masts and that way we where able, to do three performances a day! Easter Sunday came and we really made true, on what he wanted! the first performance was at ten am, after Sunday mass, then the second at two and when we moved the trailer, I was laying by the big window showing Otto, who had his VW hitched on the bus, my chocolate Easter Bunnies, true the window and he went like, he is going to come and eat them all and live nothing for me. When we reached the next Town, there was a change of plan, Otto and Peter wanted to go to Vienna, with the tractor, pass the new truck and get number plates for it, to leave the tractor, in Vienna so we can travel, everyday and make a lot of money, to go to America. Rosy was 8 moths pregnant. She was staying, in one of the trailers, in Vienna. Her baby was due, in May. I said Otto, I want to come with You, usual he always take me, because I never fall asleep and keep him up to ,but he said a flat' no, you can not come, you stay here and where would You sit, on the Tractor?"He said 'to Mamma,' Mamma please gives me my passport,' took his money and kissed me on my forehead and they left.

When I awoke in the morning, I felt very blue and went to look for wild flours, by the River and there I remember the dream I had, in the night. I sat in the very Green Grass, admits lots of flours, in all colors and there was a flatbed carriage, decorated with Flours and it moved with out Horses, Otto sat on it and waved me goodbye.

When I came back from the River, a Taxi came around the bend in it was Rosy and our favorite Uncle, Rudy (Pappas older Brother). I was running toward the taxi, then I see tears, streaming down the face of my Uncle and he said 'our boy is death, they drove over his head!'

It was like someone had tipped me in Ice, I stopped in my tracks. I could not talk, I was stiff. All of us pile in the taxi and left for Vienna. On the way to Vienna , uncle Rudy told us that a drunk Driver, dry to overtake Otto and drove smack into him, with such a force that the back axel and transmission, broke in the middle. On impact, it broke Otto's back to and the tractor spun around 80 degrees, Otto fell on the street and knocked the back, of his head open and then the big Wheel of the tractor, landed on his chest. He died three deaths. Peter was catapulted true the air and landed on the tracks of the tram, he was unconscious in hospital.

The accident happened at 00.05 hours, on Easter Monday 1963. Otto was twenty Years and ten Days old. Mamma said Otto should have been, her lucky child, because he was born, on an Easter Sunday, but she was wrong. The police, came at four o clock in the morning, to Rosy and ask her name and when she said, her name was Ottinis, they said her husband is Death in a crash, when Rosy fainted, they realize she was pregnant and said that they where sorry. Even then she had to come to the police station to make, identification. When she came to the police station, Otto's murderer sat there. He only had a bloody noose, Rosy dry to crab him by the treat, but Police won't let her. After that Rosy called Uncle Rudy and he came for her. When we almost reached Vienna, we saw our tractor, lying on his side, next to the road. We did not stop and went street home. There was our Dog, Mucky hounding and crying, we had left him with Rosy to protect her and he knows what had happened. All our relatives came, one by one, Rosy had to finish, the new costumes and carry one, to the Morgue for Otto, also she had to pick up his bloody clothes, there was only one shoe, the second shoe, was never found. Rosy made all funeral arraigments and had the invitations, printed and send. I don't know how she did that, or where she got the strength for it. Daddy was real drunk, every Day and he was suddenly, an old man.

Mamma was crying, without a break, I was like paralyzed, I could not eat. Mamma said,' let's turn on the gas and be done with it. ''I said and what about, Billy and Melly?'I had the same feeling as she, I also wanted to die, but something just would not let me. I was totally, disgusted with my Father, why he had to get trunk, every day, didn't we have enough problems? I just kept thinking, how my poor Brother had died on the street like a Dog and how he must be disfigured. Why did God have to do that, if there is a God? My Live was over too. I was breathing, but I was like a zombie, I still had not eaten when the Funeral came after two weeks. Of Corse my mother, bought me now mourning clothes and I had to wear, a black and white 2 Piece suit, Rosy had brought for me from America. I shaved my hair short, like a matchstick length and it matched my Mood. Not there.

The funeral was in Stammersdorf and when we get there, there where hundreds of people, our relatives and Otto's friends, everyone was crying, man and woman alike. Uncle Adie embraced me and kissed me patting my back. Someone said he is lying in the big hall, in an open coffin and I said I want to see my Brother!'Mamma wanted to hold me back, but I went anyway, no one could hold me and there he was. In an open coffin, in a Glass Box where you could not touch him; with six big Candles on either side of the glass. He looked like a Prince so beautiful it is Haunting me to this Day, like he was sleeping ,rosy cheeks his long brown eyelashes casting a shadow, on his so very handsome face, the only give away, there was a little blood, on the pillow where the back of his head was. Then my tears started to flow and our cousins where standing across the isle by the service they cried just kike me shaking and shivering. Melly and Billy walked just behind the preacher and then me alone, nobody to comfort me and that's how it remained for me. Taft, he was a family friend and a very good Illusionist, as well as a Magician, delivered the last words, on the grave site, up to this day, I don't know, what he said, there was a see of people and I don't know, who was there ,lots of people shake my hand and told me there condolences, I don't know who, I had to gather all my strength not to break down, as the flours and earth buried my brother, my happiness and my future, went in this Grave and it is still there.

As we returned home, all of us, where like not there anymore, nobody functioned, we where just hanging on to sanity.

Uncle Rudy used to come every weekend, he stayed home to, and nobody wanted to see, the suffering.I still Did not go to school, Rosy told them what happened and that I can not attend, the Director send a note to my mother to come and see her. Mamma went with me and the director, was very nice and my mathematic teacher was there to and both of them told Mamma, to let me have an education and not take me out of school, because they said, „she is the best pupil we got and we don't want to loose her.“

Please missies' Ottinis don't take her out of school, she needs an education." "No Mamma said, we are circus artists, we got no need for school." "Then can we, at least send her on a school vacation, for a month she looks sick and need to gain some weight!' bless there heart, they where more concerned for me than Mamma. She agreed to let me go and I thanked them and they wished me goods speed. The following week, I was send away to Steiermark, in the mountains, I don't remember the name, but the vacation home was in the woods. A vacation home for school the children. I think we were, about 50 or so boys and girls all my age group and we slept in a dorm, eight Girls. We spend our every day in the woods, in the crisp mountain air, collecting blue berries and tiny little strawberries.

I made several friends and pretended nothing had happened and I would stay away, from my family, for god, like I got no family. The made me eat my food and before I did not finish it, I could not leave the table, so I eat it all, except once, we had sour caly flour, I had a plastic bag in my shorts, for the berries and I but the food in it and then in my shorts pocket, the other children, flatten it on the plaid and put one atop the other. Aunty Isle saw it and made them eat it up. That must have been nasty. We played games and I was contended, until Sunday we had to go to church, in the church, I smelled the weirauch and I passed out. When I awoke, I was outside the church, on the grass and aunty Isle, was putting a cold wet cloth, on my head and pulse, she was very afraid, what had happened and told me, that I passed out and fell to the floor. After that, I was made stay home, when the others, went to church on Sundays. I was very glad, because, I did not like good anymore; he had taken Otto away from me. The four weeks where over too soon and I was afraid, what I would encounter, when I came home, would Mamma still cry all day? I was afraid, to go home. We all had to go on the scale and I had gained two pounds in one month. And then it was, going home, I know when I was gone, they became a flat, not to far from where I grow up and my sister Rosy had given birth, on the 18.of may to a baby girl name Gina Nina. We said our goodbyes, in the train and promised to stay in contact, but we never did.

Mamma was on the train station, waiting for me. She looked good she was slim, wearing a black pencil skirt and a pale blue, mohair Jacked and a blouse. It was mid June and she had put on lipstick and her hair was made up, she looked real beautiful and was not crying. I was relived. We had to go in a taxi, because it was a half hour walk from the tram to our new flat. Rosy was home with the baby.

Melly and Billy were outside playing with their new friends. The flat was big, an entrance room, a toilet, kitchen and next to the kitchen was a bath, all with terrazzo floors, a big living room and three bed rooms, with parquet floors. The flat was just one flight of stairs up and was in a very green aria. They had sold everything we had. Except for one trailer and the equipments for the act. There was some nasty people living there, they would take the mouth guard, of our dog and call the police. We had so many citations, Mamma had to give, our sweet mucky away. I don't know what became of him. They also beat, my little brother and when Mamma said to live him alone, the call her, an old gipsy whore. When I heard that I got very angry and told them to stop, or they will have to deal with me. They just laughed at me. Apart from this primitive people, all was quiet, until in July, I looked out the widow and see Mamma coming home, crying and shivering. I could not imagine why,

I said 'Mamma what is the matter, why are you crying so hard?" she said, "My sister Kristy, fell of the trapeze and broke her neck, yesterday! She is death.' between sobs, Mamma told us all the bad details. Kristy's husband, had a woman and came back, to late for performance, he had no time, to inspect the equipment, not even change to his costume and when they drove up, with the motorcycle, there was a steel wire in there path, the wire was literally invisible, in the spot lights. The ringmaster had forgotten to remove it; it was from the preceding act. Kristy's husband was as the boss, from the act and should have inspected, the equipment, before going up. So the went up, riding the motorcycle and Kristy on the trapeze behind her our cousin Ron. She was first, so the wire, struck her across her face, and Ron could not catch her, so she fell to her death. She was only 33 years old. In Just three months, we lost the most beautiful people in our family, true other people fault and you can name this also a murder. Cousin Kandy sat in the ring and saw her mother dying, never before did she perform, only after the death, of her Mother did she start to perform, together with the woman who, wrecked her family. After the accident they tied, Ron up and put him in the cellar, of the house and beat him with a leather whip, they said all was his fault, but it was not true, would they have taken Otto, this could never happen at least he would have held Kathy and she would not fall. If they would have, only taken Otto to America, both would be alive. Now mamma sat in the rocking chair, day in day out and cried and cried until she had no skin in her face. It was horrible. Mamma started to bleed and had an operation, so I did all the work at home. Then one Day, I walked home from the dentist, somebody hold my arms from behind and then I see one of the tree brothers, who always cuss my mother and beat my brother, punch me on my mouth, the tree brothers run away fast, the blood was running down my lips and I was shaking, with a rage, what do they want from us? Kill my Brother make us give away our dog cuss my Mother what are we? We are not human? My father was in Stalingrad and had the iron cross; he gave his youth and health to Austria and its nasty people. This people treated us like dirt? Mamma lost, three children wasn't that enough? The Nazis are still around; they can never get rid of them. Here they are the proletariat and the Nazis trying to destroy us completely, have we not suffered enough? I went home, my mother ask me what happened, I could not answer to her, I was not able to talk, I take off my coat and my shoes and took, the same rug beater, my mother used to beat me with, off the close rack, in the front room and went out, in the hall way, the first of them came in the house. The others saw me, true the glass next to the entrance door and stayed outside, the first was little taller than me and square, when he realize, he is alone with me, he dry to run from me, up the stairs, I follow on his heels and beat him very bad, over his head and anywhere I could get him, I had the rug beater upside down, I was holding on to the pretzel and beat him with the stick, witch had the same effect, as a police stick ,he managed to get in his front door and then, I went back down, just in time, to beat the second one, of the twins. He was about six feet tall, but I scared the shit out of him and beat him to a bulb, he was also running up. The third one, who punched me on the lip, went for the super, for help and came in the door behind the super. If he wanted to go home, he had to pass me. I was standing in front of my door. The super, a huge fatso, walked toward me, like a sumo wrestler and the coward bastard, hiding behind him. I extend my left hand, still holding on to the rug beater, with my right hand and slap the little bastard in his face, the super in turn, slaps me in my face, and then I started to beat the crap out of the super. Until finally my father came and take over, the super for me, wile my father beat up the super, I literally, beat the shit out of this proletarian bastard, I beat him so long, until I was tired, I just wanted blood, I was thirsty for it. When I finally come to my senses, there was another super, from house number Four, we where number one. The man said ,' mister Ottinis let me congratulate you, to your daughter, this is a great girl ,this fat bastard fondled my daughter, while he was supposed, to give her German lessons and dried to rape her! Don't worry about a thing, he got what he deserved and I will be your witness in court! The man was true to his word and he was great, when the police arrived he told them that the boys had beaten me, at the same time the Ambulance came four the super and the 3 brothers.

For a wile all was quiet and then the court case, for my brother came up and all the wounds opened up again. Dad and Mother had to face the murderer, in court and he only gets 1 Year in prison. On damages we only get the damaged vehicle that was 20.000 shilling and nothing else. Because Otto was not married and had no children and he was death, he don't need anything,' so what about our act? He was our breadwinner "Daddy said to the Judge," no, these dos not count, the Judge said."And so we get no reparation. Things like that can only happen in Austria and its ignorant people. Mamma was ill again and had surgery again. At this time I asked Mother to let me learn cosmetologist and she said no, we got no money. So I started to work, in the same company, as Rosy. They manufactured shampoos, perms, Hair Spray and all sorts of grooming products. The colleges there, where not so primitive, as our neighbors, but, my heart was bleeding, what had become of my live? Mother had to have a hysterectomy and this time, I had to stay home with her, because she could not carry anything. Mother was home for three weeks, still not recovered, but out of bed, when I had to go shopping and took eight year old Billy with me, on the way back, we see one of our neighbors, chatting with someone, who must have been leaving, in the same building complex as us. The neighbor was a young woman, but very primitive and uneducated, she also was ugly and we suspected here to play sex games with the boys, that I beat up some time ago. She was about twenty seven years old. When she sees us, her Sais to the other woman, loud so we could hear her," this is the low lives, who think they can beat up anyone, my Brother was a little boy, but he was no fool and he said 'if you want to see low livers, look by your own door."I just pulled his hand and said' hush up." When we came home, I said nothing to Mother, I wanted no more troubles. When I unpack the crockery's, the doorbell rings and I hear Mother going to open, then I hear a very loud boom, on the door and Mother, calling, 'Nundl come, she kicked me on my shin and also in the door, the proletarian whore." Mother said, while she pulled the bitch, by her Hair and throw she on the ground, so I had to take over, Mother was still sick. "Mother closes the door. I said and then , I beat the crap, out of her, I had such an anger in me, it eat me up, her hair flow true the apartment, we found it in the back room later. I just beat her with closet fists and pulled out her hair, as much as I could, when I got tired I said, 'Mother opens the door." "Now you whore go out, but she was holding on to the doorframe, I said if you don't go out, I have to kill you. She started screaming for help, she was hoping somebody would come. So I took up her wooden shoes and beat her over the head with it and kicked her, in her pussy, pride her fingers, of the doorframe and finally throw her out. She run up the stairs and said, "Wait when my husband comes, he will get you!" "No problem, I said just send the "frig", I beat him to." The ambulance came for her to and the police question us, what transpired I told them she came in our apartment and attacked my sick Mother, which had not recovered from surgery. Not long after, all the men from the house, where going to attack Mother and I. They dry to kick down our door, seven grown Men, Dad was not home and in the whole aria, where no telephone, just the phone box, I told Mother to take a good weapon and I will call the police. So I had to jump out the back window and call the police, from the phone box. The squad car came and warned them, to stay away from us. After that the fatso super, from our house, started to collect, signatures, from all the neighbors, to have us evicted Mother Dad and I where called to court. The judge looked me up and down; I was still a little girl and questioned me. So I explained, that my brother was killed and my aunt, that we had to give our lovely dog away, how the cuss my mother and beat my little brother and me at last and that I had turned the tables on them. So the judge was smiling at me and said,' so you are the Head of the family then? And I said.' „Yes my lord". The judge 'made the ruling that the others will have to move out, if they don't allow us, to leave in freedom. The super lost his job and was evicted of the house. We were so happy, finally a victory.

Christmas was so depressing; it was not easy to bear. In January just before my fifteenth birthday, I was so stupid, to start to work, in an electronics factory. Just because a friend of mine was bugging me to join her there. I awoke at 4 am and left the house, without breakfast. I had to walk to the tram a half hour and then travel across town for one and a half hour and then walk another half hours, to reach work at 7 am. Then I had to carry the mail, to all the offices and was all day on my feet, except for a fifteen minute break at nine am and a half hour, lunch break. At four o clock, I finished work and reached home at 7 pm 5 Days a week, when I came home from work, there was no food left for me. So I had to eat the lousy food, in the cafeteria. All the women where hostile against me, I could see the where jealous at me. The men, where extremely courteous, to me, I know, they wanted to date me. I had very shiny dark blond hair, cut like an Egypt Queen, green eyes, a prominent nose, oval face, full lips, and an hour glass figure and legs like Marilyn Monroe. I could have worked as a model. But thanks to my Mother I was a factory worker. I would pass out, maybe once a month, before I get my period and then the rumors where flying, that I was pregnant. I hated the behavior, of this people and I did not now, how to cope, when I come home, no food and no one to talk to. Saturdays, I had to scrub, all the floors, with steal wool, then vacuum the dust and wax the floor after this, there was a heavy brush and I had to shine the floor, with it. When I finished I was exhausted. My mother was the bad stepmother from Cinderella and my Sister and brother where the stepsisters. They eat all the food and mess up the apartment real bad, nobody cared. Not even my Dad. The friend, who told me, about the Factory, lived in the same apartment complex, as I and I went out with her on Sundays. I had to be home by 8 pm, soon my friend Trudy had a boy friend, and he was electrician, trainee in the factory. He had a friend, who was also a trainee and we went on double dates. They also had a band and always played on the Saturdays. I was not so interested, in boys, but I had no one else. All of them where smoking and when ever, I was blue and cried they gave me cigarettes and soon I was a smoker. My boy friends name was Franz; he took me to his parents. They where nice and his mother, was a short round woman, blond and blue eyes. She was from Germany and always stuffed me with food, his father was a tall man, dark blond curly hair blue eyes and always very nice to me. They where more interested in me than my own family. The apartment they lived in, had a kitchen where you enter and then a living room, master bedroom rolled into one, Franz shared a small cabinet, with his two brothers and one sister, the toilet and water, was outside the apartment and was used by two more families, This was even worst as we had it, in the trailers. His mother worked as a cleaner and his Father had a manager position, by the state telephone, he made good money. But they still lived in this lousy apartment. His father could have bought a better one. But he said he will buy a house in the country when he retires. That's the proletariat, But with my Mother giving me no comfort and cussing me all the time, calling me a skinny whore and an ugly whore. The neighbors, told anyone, that I was a whore, because my Mother said so herself. This family was a lifeline. His siblings were by far nicer to me than my own. Franz even came with me to the cemetery, to visit with my brother, which was a disaster anytime I went there. I was inconsolable and cried for hours on end. I felt like I was not alone again. In the morning he waited for me on the train station and walked with me to work and in the evening we went back, together to the train station. He had only two stops and I had a whole lot longer to go. I made 270 Schilling a week and had to give my mother 100, from the rest, I was buying my clothes and tickets for the train and the tram as well, as the food in the cafeteria. I was very unhappy. At home it was a hostile environment. Melly and Billy always made a lot of mess and I had to clean it up, soon my Mother wanted me to, wash the dishes, I said categorically 'no.' I had enough work, with the floors.

In the spring, the case came up with the boys and the super. The other super, the one which had his daughter abused, by our super. The Judge examined the evidence and questioned the Boys and the two supers and at last me, my Dad and my Mother and then he said, "we will not discuss anything, that has transpired, between this children. These actions between juveniles are not to prosecute,'but if you want me to belief, this fragile child, has hurt, you like this, you are mistaken. 'He said to the super. 'Case dismissed."We went home, with our only friend, in the apartment complex and where happy, to celebrate our victory.

The factory was so big, about 320 different departments and everywhere, I went the great me friendly and said," The girl with the beautiful hair!" I had splurged and had my Hair bobbed and once a month I bought something to dress in a boutique. Also I bought matching bags and shoes. I could afford that because Franz paid for the entertainment and we always eat by his parents. When I went out once a week, I looked good. Franz was a drummer, in a band and he would take me along on Saturday's. His friends dubbed me the Princess and some of them called me, Queen Nefertiti. But my mother still called me an ugly whore. That was the norm, deep down; I always know she never loved me.

In the summer, at work , I run in to a girl, dressing the same way as me and having the same hair style like me, blond hair and blue eyes, we could not help, but realize, that we looked like twins and we now know, why people always said,' weren't you here just a wail ago?'We know what this was about, when we met. Her name was Elisabeth and she was a non religious Jewess, we became fast friends and always went out together, in the student Clubs, away from the proletarias.The proletarians we only endured weekdays. In autumn, Elizabeth went back to school and I was still going, to the factory. I had no choice; my Mother would not support school for me. So it was factory, all the way. I always wonder if I am going there, for the rest of my live. Or what will my live be? Franz and I where going steady. We did some petting, but I was still a virgin. When the cold weather came, he went with me, to a Taylor and had him, make a heavy poncho and a matching skirt for me. I still had no winter coat. I had to wear two sweaters underneath the poncho so cold it was. I had to, walk true deep snow, going to work, in the morning, they only clean the snow at seven pm. So when I reached work, I was already exhausted. My boss was a women and like most woman she hated me, this day, when I sit down for my 15 minutes break, to eat my bread, she wanted me, to get up and go again, she said 'young girls don't need to sit" and she always accused me, that I am pregnant ,whenever I passed out. So this time, I just had it with her idiotic manners. I just refused and went street to the (betriebsrat) workers union. And my boss, she was a ugly single woman, about six foot tall and had yellow short curly hair and freckled skin , small breast and scatter teeth , was called to the office and had to apologize to me. After that I insisted the move me out of her department. The placed I right across her desk, in a class box, where I was on my own, giving out parts to different departments. It was like running a store. Finally freedom from the old bitch and no more running around so much. I had a chair and could sit more often. I realized that most of this women, working there, where not only ugly but also very stupid and the men where horny and would not do anything for me. That was the summary then, all stupid and wicked people, not very good. I just could not imagine, how my live would go, in this ugly place, with this ugly people.

The next court hearing came up, with the skinny bitch. This time the Judge realized, that I was in fact strong and muscular, he allowed self defense, but only to a sear ten degree, he said, it was evident that I acted in a kind of rage and fined me 270 schilling, a weeks pay, I said thank you your honor, it was worth it and I said to my Mother best you pay, it was all about you, my Mother paid, she liked it too. So we put all the problems, with the neighbors, behind us, after a long time of fighting. The where afraid of me and stopped all action. My sister Rosy met a Persian man and married him, after a short courtship. She took me to meet him; he was impressed with my beauty. But I never liked him; I clearly know he just married her, to get an Austrian passport. He moved in Rosés Room, but only for a very brief time, nobody liked him and Billy, would go to spy on them, when they had sex. Then they found a very cheap flat, in the 10. District, not far, from where I was working. Gina my nice was a very cute little Girl, I liked her a lot, she had to go to Kindergarten and Rosy was working, in a supermarket.

Franz was always with his band playing out, on Saturdays, always in youth centers and I would come along, with my friends, Trudy and Elisabeth. On my sixteenth birthday, I was with all of my friends and everyone brought me a Box of chocolates, I had nine boxes. When I came home, I put them on top of my Closet. That was on Sunday. On Monday I went to work and when I come home, they had eaten all my chocolates, except one single piece, they left for me. I was really angry, with my sister and brother and my mother said 'you don't love them."So I must love them, when they so disgusting and take every thing I got from me? Melly wore my silk dress, on the grass, to play princess with her girlfriend. And I have to love that? Cleaning the house for hours. And then they come home and do not take of there shoes and mess everything up? I was so fed up and hoped, to get away from them soon. It was almost, as if I don't belong to this family. Franz was not really making me happy, he was very silly. Going to work in the morning, he would trip me and then catch me, so I don't fall to the ground. After he kept tripping me, I got feed up and dripped him and did not catch him and he hit the gravel stones, with His noose and then, he never tripped me again. He always bragged with his boxing skills and showed me, how to deliver, and an upper cut. Like line up your wrist, with your fist and hit the chin strait. I said so? And hit Him on the chin, as he had showed me and he fell to the ground, as if He had no legs. When He woke up, he was very quiet, never bragging again. I was so disappointed having a silly Boy friend like this. The next thing came, when there was a Rolling Stone, Concert in Vienna. I was not really interested, but He bought expensive tickets, to the Stadthalle and we went. First where the Side show and then there was a Break, before the Stones where coming. We went to get some sodas, when we came back; somebody was in our expensive seats. So Franz looked stupid, because he was afraid to confront them. All of a sudden the riot Police was there, asking no questions, they took him out, to the side lines and I followed ,I did not know, what else to due The pushed Him on the ground and stepped on his back and without even thinking , I poured my soda, over the Guy, who stood on his back. I could not look this fast, when one of them, boxed me on my eye and four of them take me on my limps and throw me in the police car, with the cage behind, but in a very small extra cage, where I could not move and said to the other police man, „watch her she is a violent one, „now I was sixteen Years old and about 110 pds and 5 feet six inches tall and this Guys where about 6 feet ten inches and more, nothing below that ,pretending I was a danger. I was blind in one eye and when we reached the police station, I said I want a Doctor and My Dad, they asked my address and tel. number from my parents, and throw me in a cell. They left me there until 4 am and then bring me to one interrogation room and the they said 'we cannot find your parents they are not at home ,'O Yes they are at home ,my little Sister is seven and my brother is ten and they never live them alone at home!'I said. so the insist they could not find them and forced me to sign a document, what I could not read, because I could not see very good, my right Eye was swollen like a balloon and affected also my left eye, so they make me sign and send me on my way, that way I had no witness to what they did to me, on top of that I was a juvenile and they would be in big trouble. I sign, they let me go and I went Home by Tram. The same time they let me go, they call my father to come for me. That way nobody see what they did to me, that's why the throw me in the cage alone. Turns out they let Franz go home, just after one hour and he did not even call my parents. What an ass, I was so finished with Him, I wanted to break up. When I told the doctor, the police did this to me, he did not help me either and by law, he was supposed to press charges against the police. That convinced me there is still Gestapo in Austria. Well my parents did not give me any consolation and my siblings continued to terrorize me. So I had no other way, but stay with Franz, the asshole. I would call him to my self. Now I realize that I was the asshole, I should have never talk to him again, a real shit he was. In summer there was a vacation trip to Yugoslavia, very cheap, you had to sleep in a dorm together with 6 other Girls and my vacation money was enough to pay for it. Franz went to, with the boys group, prior to the vacation, he convinced me, to have sex with Him and having no real family, I gave in to Him. It was not good, wham bang and gone madam. Rather disappointing and after I was sorry I did that. But I could not chance back. This summer was just rain in Vienna and my Mother, Did not want me to go to Yugoslavia, but I insisted that I have a vacation. I would not have one for the next twenty years. The weather was very nice and the beach was not so good, it had these little animals' with pricks, like needles Franz the asshole run in the water, first and stepped at one and had to go Hospital to get the pricks out.Two weeks He could not go in the water. But I had the time of my live, the food was very good and I eat lots. Also they other Girls, where very nice and we had lots of fun together. There was the daughter of the Persian Consul and she was a blast, with her diplomatic Passport, she smuggled a whole suitcase of Cigarettes for us. When I came back home the Fun was over, it was back to the Factory and my disgusting family. Melly and Billy, where playing outside, till nine o clock and I had to be home by seven and Saturday by ten. I had much less rights, then these small children. On top of that, Mamma wanted me to wash Her Dishes, I just refused. I felt like I was a Step Child. Another strong winter came and I had to walk true the deep snow, one day, there was so much snow, the train got stuck and we had to wait, for a full hour on the cold train station, this day I get home after 8 pm and was frozen stiff, when I get home, I stood in front of the toilet and could not pull down my garments, to use the toilet, so I peed on myself. My mother was not worried about me, all she cared for was, give her the money and that's it, they did not even know, I was a smoker. They smoke so much, they did not notice.All I ever get from her was, skinny whore and no support ever and anytime Saturday come, she wants me just to work for her. I need no rest and no fun. I always have these nightmares, where I wake up screaming. One night I dream a man wants to strangle me and I wake up screaming loud. I went to my parents to sleep between them, alto there was no sleep, and they snored in my ears from both sides. One day after my seventeenth birthday, I Wanted to go out, it was Sunday. ", Mamma said you cannot go out, you need to look after the Children,'Ok I Just call and tell my friends, I will not come "I said. Mamma went ballistic, calling me a skinny whore again and telling my father that, I don't want to stay with her Children. Her Children. I am not her child? Papa comes and says 'You stay home "and slaps me in my face. I was so Hurt by this, I did nothing to deserve that and I said to my self this is enough, now She even turns papa against me, I am not tacking this. I am leaving this place, nobody loves me here. I put on my coat and take my handbag and Jump out the window, of my room. I went strait, to my Sister Rosy and ask her, if I can stay with her and she says as long as you want. There was a small apartment, in the same house maybe I could get it. My father called Franz home and told them, that he want me to come home, or he call the Police, so they tell Him, that I was with Rosy. The next day he comes to Rosy and says that I have to come home, or they will put me in a Home, for bad Girls> I said 'no problem this cant be much worse than home."Papa left and came back the next Day and said, "You merry Franz, or we give you in a Home "I said 'I don't want to get married, put me in the home. "Daddy had tears in his eyes, when he left. Then Franz parents told me, that he went by them and said that if Franz marries me, he doesn't have to put me away. Franz parents agreed, that we should marry, because they liked m, in there family. Rosy to, said" merry him, what can be worse than our parents?"I had to agree with that. So Franz and I had to go to court, because, we where not of age to get married. The Judge said Franz is not mature enough to marry, but the Girl is very level Headed, so let's give it a dry." And so we married in March 1966, three Years after my Brother died, de must have been turning in his grave. My Father in law was really nice, with his help, we get the apartment, in the house where my sister lived and his father also, furnished the apartment for us. He said he is proud, to have me as His Daughter in law, my Mother in law was also very sweet to me, she even made and appointment by her hairdresser, to pin up my long Hair, for the wedding.My parents, had given there consent before and did not attend, the wedding. They gave me nothing at all. The wedding was in city hall and my mother in law coked a nice meal for us, nobody was there Just His Parents. We took two pictures by a photographer and that was it. I was married. The wedding night was noting to Wright home about it. The apartment was not so great, but I was my own master. The toilet was inside but it had no bath. So I always used the shower, in the locker rooms in the Factory. Any time I took my clothes off, the woman started to stare at me, as if they want to kill me. They stick there heads together; they never see a pretty woman before. I don't know what I did to them. Rosy had a problem with the Persian shit head, she catches him cheating on her and he throw her out of the apartment, which was her apartment. In the middle of the night, her little Girl was tree Years old. Rosy Called me, in the middle of the night, I was staying over at my in-laws and told me the police where not helping her! they just said' that's your one problem, when you marry a foreigner!'So I get up and go to the Police. I tell them that this is scandalous and I will put this in the newspaper that my Sister is standing on the road, with her little child, because the police are not protecting her. Boy that made them angry, the went there and told Rosy husband, to get out of there and when he did not leave, they beat the crap out of him, all the furniture fall down, when the beat him and throw Him out of the apartment. Rosy was happy and He know, I did this that pissed him even moor. Rosy was happy, I could not belief, that I had to come to rescue her, still no man in the family, nobody there, except Me. My Hair was long, it graced my hips and I had some nice mini Dresses. Where ever I went, heads turned. The people in the factory where really a pain. I repeatedly I dreamed of my Brother Otto and it was so real, that I always had to believe He is alive. It was always the same Dream, and it went like this. Suddenly he would come back and I say, o you are not Death, where have, you been and why you left me alone? ",

He said' sorry I had to go. "I say' but I am Happy you are here now."He says," I am sorry but I cannot stay here." And then I awoke thinking He is alive, but after some moments of happiness I remember, he is not.

The next Year, it was my eighteenth birthday, Franz had to join the military and I took my friend Trudy as a room mate, so I wont be alone. Her boyfriend was also drafted and went to the same place as Franz. This was not a wise decision, because Trudy did not want to clean and also did not like to pay for nothing. One time we went to visit it was a disappointment, I never did it again, and I went to his parents instead on Sundays. I also started to visit with my parents again and one day, the where operating a little carnival and Pappas friend, had to give them a lift to go there. The stepdaughter, of this man was my friend and he ask my Father, If I would come for the ride, so it is not so boring for him, I think nothing bad, also not Papa and I say ok I will come, after all the man knows me ,sins I am six and has 11 children. On the way back, about 50 kilometers, away from my family, he starts to talk, he wants me, as his Girlfriend and he will buy whatever I want and he dry, to but His Hand, between my legs, all that while he is driving, I tell Him to leave me alone,' I don't want You at all, „but You are not a virgin. "' I say 'go to Your Wife and Children. "There is a lake over there, we can go skinny dipping and have sex there. „He says. I started to have a panic and said "remembers my Father, he knows that I am with you, if any thing happens to me, he will kill you." And that worked, he know, I am saying the truth, my father would kill him, and so He left me alone and did not say another word to me. The same summer there where some Artists from Germany, in Vienna and my parents went to the show with me, they where very successful, alto they could have never touched our performances. They all had big trailers and more than one Mercedes Benz. The where in Vienna several weeks and one day, I was visiting my Parents, the owner of the show, was by my Father and when I get ready, to leave he offer to give me a lift home. He was and older Man and his wife was old to, so I really did not think, that He would du me something, but he did, he drove to a road, next to the Danube River and I said," this is the wrong road, you need to turn around.' He drove to a dark parking lot and stopped the Car, I had no time to get out of the car, he pushed an electric button and I fell back with the seat and he throws himself on top of me, he man must have been a good two hundred pounds. I was so afraid, my heart started pounding in my chest, when I remember the magic words , My father will kill You, if any thing happens to me. He immediately got off me and took me home. I said never again, will I go alone in a car with a Man. When Franz came back from the military, I found an apartment, where I was the super, near by and quit my Job at the Factory ,I had have enough of this work. This Summer I was free and went almost everyday to swim and I would meet Elizabeth in the swimmbad and have nice chats with her. I told her that I was so lonely for my Brother, and she said why I don't you have a baby that would make you happy. I told her, we where not ready, for this and she said, "why not Just give it a try and when you have sex ,just hold him when he comes and then he cannot pull out.' I just started to think about, what she had said and did think I could get a boy and he could be like my Brother and the longer I was thinking about it, the more I was sure, it would be like that. So one Day in September, I did what she had said and after 3 weeks I know I was pregnant, I started to throw up, every morning and needed to buy bigger bras, every month.Still I was glowing and happy to be pregnant. I stopped smoking immediately and as I was fife months along, I was already very thick. Rosy run away with one of the artists, from the guy, who was going to rape me. She just brings Gina to our mother and said she will be back in a couple of hours. She did not come back and went to Turkey with the troupe. Mamma was floored she had to give up her Job. Jess she was working, because she had no support from me and not from Rosy. So she went to social services and they gave her money, so she could take care of Gina. Aunty rosy was working there to as a cleaner; she had lost her two Houses, because her husband was a whore monger. He mashed up the business and she went from being a business woman and her two stories House and a bungalow and a Mercedes Benz. To a little garden house as well as a small French Car. She had all her live her own business and now was a cleaner. It was hard for us. Two deaths and the rest, of us turned factory workers. I would never imagine my Mother and Aunt Rose, working as office cleaners. And last but not least I was married to an Electrician and had a Job, as a Super, what had happened to all of us? We where now, the biggest misfits ever! I was sure Otto was turning in His Grave. And now I was pregnant and was just running back to my Mother, what was I Doing? Franz also Quit the Job at the Factory, his Father had convinced him that He has better courier chances, with a Government Job and also, he can never loose His Job and will be save from economic crisis. As we had it in Austria before the big war everybody out of a Job. A number of times, I got a painfully remainder, that my Husband could not defend me at all. If tugs would molest me he laps his tail and run. In my first months of pregnancy I know, it was a bad choice to marry Him. Doom and gloom decedent up on me.

Chapter 4

4. Chapter
MOTHER HOOD! 1968

I was getting bigger and bigger and the more my pregnancy progressed, I just wanted to be with my Mother. So we moved in with her and we had the same room Rosy used to live in. Franz had to give her half His salary and she liked that. As soon as I was pregnant, Franz did not touch me again, I had the feeling, that He was disgusted of me. I disliked Him more and more. The main topic was my big belly, it was enormous, I waddled like a Duck and got sick every morning, everyone said, that they where only sick, for the first, three months, not me, I got sick all the time. From 9 am to 9pm, I just eat and drink 2 liters coca cola per day, no water; I also eat apples for the baby and stopped smoking, at once. I cleaned the big apartment myself, after my parents left Vienna, they went on tour again. Slowly they gained some form of sanity again and Billy was fourteen years old and helped, Daddy to put up the wire and also performed with Daddy and Melanie. Melanie was eleven years old, but she was as tall, as Billy and looked as old as he. They Just worked close to Vienna, Daddy had lost his strength, when Otto Jr. Died. He suddenly became an old Man. He still performed, but he had lost his vigor, every afternoon he needed to nap and Mamma did not understand that He was just worn out. At home I was just miserable, my belly, was so big and sins a Man pushed me in the tram, because I was so slow, to get in and after I realize, what he did and who did it, I went ape and Mamma had to hold me back, from killing this idiot.So when I was alone, I just stayed at home. Rosy came back home, to Austria and brought her new, Boy Friend with her. He had a Trailer and a Mercedes Benz. Our Parents had only a Tractor and so they could use him to tour with them. He could find new locations, for the high wire act. Franz liked my Parents a lot and on the weekends, he often went with me, where the where. Begin of May, we went to them. Billy was making a new trick; he hung with one foot in a strap, from the wire and would slide down the wire, very fast. When I watched Billy, he came down the wire from the church, above one roof below the church, but the wire sank and Billy hit the roof, with his head, full force. I said, "Now my little Brother is dead to."I know, Rosy friend had put up the wire and made a mistake. The Baby in my belly started to jump and I went for Anton. I was getting ready to kill him, but he must have sensed my, intentions and run away as fast as he could. Billy came off the Roof; his head was a bloody mess, but lucky, he only received, minor cuts and bruises. I had enough and stayed home for the reminder of my pregnancy. My belly button spiked out and hurt me, so I asked the Doctor every Day, if this is the Day. On Sunday the 19th of May, we went to his Parents, to eat Lunch and after, played a game of cards. At four pm, I could not sit anymore and we went Home. I watched TV in Bed and He slept. I had to go to the toilet a lot and had some bleeding. I could not sleep, I know the Baby is coming, but I also know from my Mother, that it could take about 24 Hrs toward the morning, I felt contractions, every half hr. and told Him, when He woke, that the Baby is coming and to call an ambulance for me. He said," I have to ask my Mother." I said, "Is Your Mother Having a Baby or I?"Maybe you can take the tram?"He said. I am not going with the tram, are you stupid? I can not walk a half hour and then ride the tram for a hr. you want me, to give birth in the tram?' I am not staying here alone! I give you ten minutes, to bring the Ambulance, or I call a Taxi. I had my bag packed, sins two weeks already and the ambulance came very fast. In the ambulance he sat on the stretcher and I on the bench. They drove so fast, I wonder if I would reach in one peace. **********He was not concerned at all for me; I just had no more love for him at all. I really was sorry, to have a Baby by this Idiot, with a capital I. In the Hospital, he could not wait to leave. He was going on a three Day Cruise, on the blue Danube, with His colleges. Like he did that on purpose so he had no cause, to be with me. He left before the Doctor examined me. I did not care. The Doctor looked at me and said, we will have the Baby by eleven and why did you shave? 'I said "I shave, so you don't have to shave me, I also did not eat this morning. Now that was good news for her. Non the less she gave me a irrigation, so my colon would be empty, I also took a Hot shower after that and then they put me in the labor room. For an hour I was alone there, and then at eleven still no action, I just go in and out the bathroom. At Noon a Woman comes in and when I see her, dirty feet, I throw up. From then I feel so bad, that I could not, get up again. The pain got worse and the woman asked me, if I want a banana. I said thank you but I cannot eat. One or two times, the Nurse looked at me; otherwise I was left to my self. I had trouble breathing and in a lot of pain, there and then, I never, wanted to get pregnant again.where was my Mother, nobody even ask how I was. at seven pm. the Woman next to me called the Nurse and the Nurse said ,I see the head Crowning ,Push and the woman went ,hoouuu. And the Baby was there.I saw when they clean it and but it on the scale. The Baby, it was a Girl, had 3Kilo and seventy Deka. And she was 52 Centimeter long.when they finished with the Baby, it was 8 pm, I said please I cannot breath again.' finally the Doctor came ,she was very Young.she gave me a oxygen mask and pinched the bubble , so the water broke, then I had to press and breath ,and press and breath and the fat short nurse ,would press the baby down with her arms ,but the Baby did not come for one hr.I was so exhausted ,I was thinking , I will Die ,then the Doctor said she need to cut me open and when I pressed ,the next time she cut me. Then I had to hold my legs close to my Body and the fat Nurse was pressing the Baby down ,it took fife more ,time to press and then, the Baby fell right on my Belly. they had my ass, way up in the air.I was so exhausted ,that I did not see what sex it was ,then she took the Baby by its feet and it started to cry.they said, we have a healthy Boy and he is 48 centimeter long and ways 3Kilo and Twenty   that is about six and a half pounds.after a wile ,the nurse, throw herself on me again ,to get out the after birth.when the Doctor stitched me up ,3 more Doctors came and just lean at the foot of the bed, as if they are watching TV and said to the very young Doctor not to sew to much, because my Husband would not like that.I could not believe that nasty joke ,But I was so exhausted ,II had no power to cuss them. Hold your legs still, she said, but I could not, I was just shaking with exhaustion and my legs, where strapped to the stirrups they where jiggling like a pudding. I was 29 hours in Labor. when I was ready ,the nurse gave me some Soup and I had to decline I could not drink it.at two am, the brought me to a Room and we where six Women there.when they brought my Baby ,I saw Him for the first time ,I was shaking with fear and started to cry uncontrollably. he had one eye completely swollen shut and the other half way ,the ends of His ears where bend and his noose to and there was a big pump on his head ,He looked disfigured.the nurse came and said to stop crying ,He was ok and in two weeks he would look normal I did not stop for hrs.and then my skin started to itch ,so bad, I could not sleep and my belly was black and blue.In the afternoon the visitors came ,I had none.so I went to tell , my two friends that I had a Baby Boy ,they where delighted and said they will visit soon.In the Night ,I was walking up and down the hallways my skin rash got worse And itched me so that I could not sleep .In the morning ,the Nurse brought my Baby and His mouth was so small ,that my nipples could not fit ,so the Nurse squeezed my nipple and said so you have to do it. I said you hurting me and slapped Her Hand very hard," don't touch me again I said to Her".I raised my two Siblings ,I don't need you, to tell me what to do.after that my Son started to Just kiss my nipple very loud and did not drink at all.all the woman was breaking up over Him. they laved so loud, that was the great entertainment.So they gave me a pump and I had to pump the milk and feed Him with the bottle.One time I drink the soup they gave me and I got so much milk I had to get up at two am to pump milk again.what a drag I absolutely could not get enough sleep.I stopped to drink soup. they gave me calcium injections and they made me sleep, always when my baby came ,I was asleep.so I told them, not to give me ani ,injektions again. they where so stupid in this Hospital unbelievable.after my Son was four days old ,his Daddy came and brought Me some cheap flours ,the where so small and funny looking ,definitely ,not Roses. I don't even touch them, they other women, where busy, so they did not see the flours.I was glad nobody knows they are for Me, I was so ashamed. later after the visitors left they said ,look at this flours who they belong to ?I said nothing at all. on Saturday my grandma came and she brought me ,a very pretty gold ring with a Perl and diamonds ,my husband stole it from me later.also She brought me, a compote of apples ,because I was hardbound and the wound hurt Me ,Grandma was still a very good looking Lady she was in her seventies white hair and white skin dark eyes.she wore a wide brim black hat a two pike suit and looked like a Countess. as usual she had Her nice jewels on and she looked very nice ,I was very proud of Her and surprised that she visit me.She   said ,the rash is from the bed sheets and from the harsh chemicals they are washing them.she told me ,that she always had the same in Hospital. at home it would just go away.after all My Grandma looked out for Me.I really needed that and I was happy she came ,My Friends also visited with me and brought Me long stemmed Red Roses.on Monday the Doctor said, You need to go, to have Your skin looked after ,they Nurse there on the skin ward ,looked at me like I had a desise and said ,"You need to stay here and the Baby stays at the maternity ward" ,"no way ,"I said ",I am going home today ,with my Baby" ".but You know you will have to sign a waiver, that we are not responsible, if anything happens to You ' she said"."No problem I am of legal age." I said.Franz came to pick me up in a Taxi.I was glad I where going home. my Father in law had bought Me, a nice Baby Pram blue and with little curtains and a Baby Bed.He was really good to Us.My rash just vanished, as Grandma said it would.But still I got not enough sleep this neighbors where a real drag they made so much noise.I sat for hours to just look at my Baby.He was so sweet and I worried about Him a lot. everyday I walked with Him in the pram. His father was never at home he said he is working; I did not miss Him at all.I cried a lot I was worried, what will become of my Son, in his live. once in a wile ,we would visit my parents ,as they where ,performing.it was a sad , troupe Papa was performing as good as ever , but He was not Him self anymore , before He was a sparkling personality ,now He was subdued. We all where like zombies there was a big open wound in us and it never healed. Billy and Melanie grow up in a sad environment.I could not bear to go back there. Autumn came and My Parents returned home.My Dad found a town House for us and we bought it very cheaply, it had a little Garden but no bath or shower ,just a toilet ,kitchen ,living and two bedrooms ,I was not happy but I had to enroll my little Boy ,to kinder garden ,I needed to go to work ,so we could fix the House. there where some furniture in the House and a big oven in the Kitchen ,where we cold heat the kitchen and the small bedroom.no hot water.I found a job in a wholesale 45 minutes walk from us.it was December when I started there.I had to wake my Son at fife in the morning ,he wanted to sleep longer, but I had to bring Him to kinder garden at six.as soon as I drop Him ,I run to reach work at seven. My college was a 40 Year old woman who behaved like she is seventy.I just had to stand on the ladder and all the guys ,including the boss , try to look under my skirts ,but under need I wore long thick underpants.so nobody see nothing at all.still the peeping toms never give up. I earned more money there, but after paying for the kinder garden, utilities, coal, for the oven rent and food there was no money left, Franz did not give me any money at all. He said He is working overtime and saving the money to fix the house.He was hardly ever at home.At 1600 hr.I got of work and had to run Home because the kinder garden closed at 1700 hrs.my poor Baby was always last to be picked up.and I kissed and cuddled Him a lot every time I Picked Him up.with Him on My arms I had to run to the shop to by groceries and when we reached home ,I was exhausted.I had to split wood and start a fire ,put a big pot with water on the oven ,while it get warmer I would cook our food then feed the Baby and give him his bath and put Him to Bed.by the time I had washed his tapers and cleaned the apartment and myself it was 2200 hrs. no Husband at home day in day out.once in a blue moon He would come home early and want to have sex ,which I did not want. I had totally lost all my feelings for Him and I told Him to live me alone.in cold day in January, the snow was knee deep , my great husband was at home ,my baby started a very high temperature.I told Him to call a Doctor ,but the lazy ass did nothing ,I was afraid to leave my child with him and it was dark outside ,so I told him, to go to the phone boot. But he did not. all off a sudden the baby went blue ,he had passed out and he was stiff as a board ,I drought He was death.I was screaming at Him to get a Doctor , instant and then He finally went for one ,I was scared to death ,after a wile ,I cant say how long ,my Baby woke up and his color came back ,that was when the Doctor arrived.He looked at the Baby and said nothing wrong with Him.I said this cannot be true He has a very high temperature.He said no he is good and left ,without giving me any medication for the child.,' I said get the Taxi or I kill You ".finally He did what I said.when we arrived at the Children's Hospital ,My Baby was immediately admitted ,He was very Ill ,He had ,had a cramp ,from His high Temperature and a Tonsillitis. He could have died. With a very heavy heart ,I had to leave my Baby there.I was finished with my Husband ,when I gave birth , but now I was totally finished and feed up with His sorry ass.He gave me no support at all ,no money all He wanted to do is ,fuck me and I did not need this.I needed to get rid of Him as soon as possible.I had to work and could only see my Son ,on Saturday and Sunday.No one else went to see my poor Baby.He was barley 8 months old and sick for the second time.when I held Him he was so sweet ,always smiling at me. With his big blue eyes and rosy cheeks, He looked like an angel.

When this Guys at work ,bothered me again I went out with one of them ,He was not hansom and he was also married ,but I was just doing this to get back at Franz ,until I figure it out how to get rid of Him.I had sex with the guy two times and then I said , it is not worth the effort and immediately when I get my Baby back from the Hospital ,I stopped seeing the Guy.I don't remember His name.when my Baby was home the old pattern , had started again and Franz was not coming home ,I went to driving school and this cost me an arm and a leg.Franz had to give me money to help me out.the Boss from the wholesale was behind me to and He was uglier, than the Guy before and also married to an ugly fat unfriendly woman.He was also an ex Police and I wanted no part of Him. All the time He was riding His bicycle up and down the wholesale and only stopping to look under my skirt. To hear the name Cop ,made me to recoil ,the where the worst of them all.And when he bothered me again ,I said,' I quit ,give me my papers ,'no' He said ,you are my best worker ,' I don't give You the papers.' All ride I said to my self 'fuck the papers '.I never went Back to work for two weeks and then He send me a blue letter ,I was Dismissed and He had to give me my money, including the two weeks ,I was not working .I already had a Job next door, there was also a wholesaler and I got the washing soap section.the work was very heavy ,I had to lift the big boxes with laundry soap ,it was not easy.just before my driving test ,I was supposed to pay 1000 Schilling and when I took my handbag out of the locker there was no money in my Bag ,when I told them that my money was gone they did not belief me.I said I really cant deal with this thieving assholes and quit again.After that I Took a job, by one of Vienna's biggest clothing wholesalers.because it was close to driving school. the Boss was a very short Man almost a Dwarf ,but He was rich and that's way He could afford a lot of woman.He and His brother in law started to peep under my skirts immediately.I said dam them ,they are worst than the people in the factory. the lunch room was controlled by a almost blind aunt of them and she would shave of Your lunchtime, at the least ten minutes.In the breakfast room there was no chair left for me ,so I had to spend my Lunch at the Coffee House.I graduated Driving school and quit my Job again ,when my parents asked me ,to come with them to Finland to the Circus !Rosy went to Germany with her boyfriend and they needed me.Franz liked that He took a loan and Bought a Truck for my Parents ,to go to Finland.My Dad had only a Motorcycle and Tractor Driving Permit ,so I had to drive the two and a half ton Truck hitching a small Trailer behind and with the masts on top of the Roof loaded ,it was a big load to carry. My first Drive out took me all the way to the North Sea.

We drove over the west autobahn to Salzburg ,Munich and then over the roen .the roen is about 800 km ,autobahn, just true hills and the truck is a Diesel Truck ,it was so slow you could walk next to it.mamma Just wanted me to drive ,because Daddy ,was not a save Driver ,She said.Mamma was inside the Truck with Melly, Billy and my Baby Boy, He was eleven months old. Mamma was chain smoking so nervous she was and my Baby took one of her cigarettes and eats it, He spit and spit there was no water so mamma gave Him black coffee to drink. That must have been very healthy. I drove fife Days until we reached Travemuende and but the Truck on the Ferry to Finland. the weather was nice and warm the floors and Trees where blossoming, it was Easter.our Cabins where under deck, I had a cabin with My Sister Melly and when I went with my Baby to give Him a Bath a bearded Finn, cased me all over the place ,so I run to my Parents Cabin and slammed the cabin Door behind me ,the Guy in hot perused opened the Door ,he was shocked when he saw my parents ,and the cabin full of smoke ,You could have cut the smoke with a knife ,so much it was.Well at least I got rid of Him. The food was very good and plenty, but in the night we had some ruff seas, it was terrible.we finally fell asleep, exhausted at around four in the morning.when we get up for breakfast ,Mamma' said did you hear the alarm ?"No we where sleeping!'Papa and Billy went out ,with there life saver west's on, just wearing the Pajamas and I stayed in Bed, Because I would rather drown in bed where it is warm ,than go outside in the cold ',Mamma said.I said ,'yea and we would have drowned like the rats, because You did not warn Us.'but I was glad no one woke Us, so we got a little sleep.I was seasick and had to stay on Deck all the time.I Just took some of the heavy blankets and stayed in the fresh air.when we arrived in Helsinki the sea was frozen over ,I cant even begin to describe the horror we felt.after arriving at the Circus we realized that we had to perform open air ,in this cold weather in our flimsy costumes and the Trailer was so cold we could not sleep in the night.then we found out that the payment was so low we could not leave from it ,this idiotic manager did not know what he did.the food in Finland was also not what we wanted.So Papa went to the Circus Director and told Him that this was a complete miss understanding of our Contract and that the weather is to cold also. Thank Good, the Director   let us out of the contract. the very next day we where back on the Ferry to Germany.we all where so relived, to arrive in Germany and the first thing we did, was shop for a nice side of Ham, potatoes and a salad.that was a feast.So we hit the road again 5 Days later we where in Austria and started to perform in Amstetten. Papa was in a bad mood all the time and told me every turn, I had to make , with the Truck and to top it all off ,they gave me not a penny and also did not pay, the installments for the Truck.So I told them that I go Home.when I reach home it was dark already und the door locked ,nobody home.So I called by my in laws ,He was not there ,when I go back from the phone boot ,a Car pulled up and it is ,My stupid Husband with a fat woman.He was flustered ,this is his college and she just bring him Home. I doughty nothing of it, I was definitely not Jealous. I started to hang out with my one and only childhood Friend ,Rosie.the same Guy who made the botched Contract for us ,came to Franz ,and asked Him to lend Him some money and He would give Him this little Car as security ,I told Him that the Car, is worth nothing and Franz should not lend Him Money.But He did it anyway ,Franz was working for the Vienna Public Works and had a steady rising Income ,a very good salary.I could not belief ,I was married to this ass he never gave me money but he lend this con man six thousand Schilling.As I said ,Franz never got the money back and I was stuck with the car.You put your foot on the gas Pedal and there was almost nothing. one day He made me so angry and said, the Car is good , but You cannot drive.I let the clutch go and the Car shut forward so hard ,that His seat Brooke up and He fell Backward.the next time ,he was holding the baby and I drove and he said '' cant You drive faster ?' I said not with this shit; and get out of the Car and took the tram Home, about a month and the Car was finished, no repair possible.My Dad found a cheap car for me and it was also driving, so I went out to help them on the weekends and Franz was taking care of the child.at times I would come home after midnight and he was not at Home, when I call His Parents they say, that He is on His way. Then He turn up with the taxi , the Child sleeping in his arms.the money the give me was not much ,but I Liked it better ,than working with one of this crazy wholesalers.Ronny would get sick all the time ,But I learned My lesson and always got His medicine handy for Him and never gave Him anything cold.He also had a fimose and needed to have the foreskin on His penis removed because of that.But I did not want Him in hospital if not necessary ,so I found a Hospital who would do the Surgery ambulant ,It was the Wilhelmienen Spital and I made an reservation for the surgery because they sayd it is better to do it by a small child.On the Date I went with Him and it was over in ten minutes ,they But Him in a Room and I was staying there with Him. He was very Good, He never cried and in the earning we went Home All Summer! Had to be very carful with my Son that He would not ketch a Cold.on weekends we always went to my patents to help and in autumn I took a Job as a delivery Driver.that was no good when winter approached because of snow and ice. I found a Job at a Dry cleaners and they cave me on the Job Training as a dry cleaner and I had to Iron Pants and Suits as well as Shirts , that was a very hard work ,the heat in this place was like a Sauna , but they paid me good and nobody bothered me , so I stayed.My shitty Husband still did not give me any money and He was still not spending time with Us ,so I decided it is time for a divorce.My Sons turned 3 on May 20ᵗʰ and I had to bring Him to the Hospital for His Surgery ,with relief that this problem would be over ,all the time I had too keep working to support us.on the second Day of his Surgery I came to the Hospital to pick Him up and running to His room I see Him in another Room to my left and sitting up in bed and making a very sad face when He doubt I don't com for Him ,I turn around ,as I realize He was in a different Room as where I Dropped Him off.I could see despair lifting off His Little Heart when the Nurse said 'yes Ronny You can leave Your bed now ,You are going Home with Your Mammy.before I reach Him He was out of His Bed and getting in His slippers ,I bend down to Him and pick Him Up and we hugged and kissed in between putting on His Clothes.In the Bus he had His arms around my Neck and He did not let me Go for the Whole afternoon ,when we came Home I asked Him if He is Hungry and He said yes "I want a Wurstsemmel ,'that is a white bread and a Vienna sausage ,I was afraid this would hurt Him but it was allright.To celebrate He also got the first Ice Cream in His live and He just loved it and so did I ,the fear about the fieber was over, the tonsils where out. the next day I had to take Him with me to work.I could not bring Him to nobody.Ronny was in his pram and he was very happy to be with me.after one week I had to bring Him back to Kinder Garden.and then I confronted His Daddy and told Him that ,I want a divorce ,I am always alone and get no money I don't need that ,I told Him ,immediately He wanted to take me out on Sunday and His mother would have Ronny over night.I did not want to go but He said He already made all the arraignments and His College would go with Us.we went to the Chattanooga there was a live Band and it was very entertaining. He said that it could be that he will have to go to work early ,but in this case George that was his College would take me to Neusiedlersee, that is a Lake on the Hungarian Border and was before belonging to Hung aria.Shore enough He comes back and says that Yes He got to work.I was looking forward to have a day out and we went to pick up Ronny and bring Him to the Kinder Garden and we would be back in the evening for Him.George had a New Car and He let me sleep in the back ,because we where up all night.when we reach the Lake we met other friends there and went to sleep in the shade until noon. we had a nice Lunch on the Restaurant and after a good Swim.George was not good looking at all ,He was short like me ,fat and tinning Hair but he had very gentile manners and big brown Eyes. He told me about His family in Greece and that He had two Children with His Wife and that he will go back as soon as He get His Engendering Diploma.Until this time He would be working as a night watch Man at the same place as my Husband.On the way back He let me drive His Car and all of a sudden He wanted Me to pull over by the Gas station. He said I have to tell You something and I hope that You will not, be angry with me.I was puzzled as to what He Had to Say and I told Him to go on and here is the story ,He said.'Your Husband has another Woman, ever sins You got Pregnant and he goes out with Her all the time.when You gave birth ,He was on a Cruise with Her and He goes Dancing with Her all the time ,she works at the same place as He and He has Sex there with Her while I watch Your little Boy last time He was Crying and I had to urge Him to go Home with the Child ,I don't know what He want with Her but He has Sex with her all the time the are like Rabbits and She is Ugly and ten Years older than Him. You are a Goddess ,I don't know How He can Cheat on You with Her !He wants me to sleep with You now ,so He can Go out with Her !I am sorry I had to tell You But He ruins Your Live.You deserve much better than Him !Please don't be upset ,I don't want You to bee unhappy.I said' George How Can I bee upset with You ?I wanted a Divorce from Him a long time and I don't love Him anymore ,the only thing I ask of you Please go and Confront Him with me and bear witness if I need it By the Divorce. He agreed and went home with me ,Franz was already home with my little Boy and when we confronted Him he wanted to refuse to divorce me and I told Him that His Girlfriend will go to Prison for six months ,if he dos not agree with the Divorce.I told him that I will go immediately to my parents and file for divorce.I Pack up our clothes and George brought me and Ronny to my Parents. they where surprised at the news ,but not to upset.George explained to my Parents what Franz did and my Mother said that' Franz ,always complained about Nundy , that She cant cook and Houshold',George said " non of it is true ,I would thank God daily If I had a Wife like Her ,but I am married with Children and I could not ask Her '.The next day I went back to Vienna ,quit my Job and started Divorce preceding.we agreed to go whiteout Attorneys.It was Summer and we went to all divergent fests with our little carnival and from Day one my Dad wanted to fix me up with a Man. He would bring them and Say this is so and so and he is Single.I say' Daddy stop you embarrass me, I am not looking.' But you need a Man who looks out for you and the Boy! And the next Day He would bring another suitor again. My little Brother Billy was also worried about me and said 'what are we going to do now?'He was so nice and I felt at home after a long time alone.

Chapter 5

THE BEAST HAS ARRIVED. 1972 revised !!! Chapter 5

I was twenty three years old and had a three year old son, no money and no husband. I did not worry too much, I know my daddy, would look out for me. We where on a fest, next to the woods, begin of August and when we but up our little carnival business, there was a stand with cream puffs and ginger bread and toys and a stand, which sold French fries. Daddy liked to eat French fries and was always going there, to buy fries, after a wile, I see how daddy chats with them and also drink wine with the guys, a huge fat guy and a redheaded slim guy. I paid them no attention, until daddy started his game again and told me, that the slim one, was a business man and was interested in me and I should size the opportunity. He wanted to invite me to the restaurant on Sunday after we closed. I told my dad, that I was not interested. After a wile, I see the redhead watching me. Later on, the fat man came to me and the fat man said, his name was Ed and his brother in law was Walt. Walt has fallen head over heals for me and was to shy, to ask me out, to the restaurant with them. I said what the heck; I am saving myself for what? And so I went, Walt was not saying much and we had a dinner and danced a bit and before we went in the car he started kissing me and said if I could drive, we could drop off Ed and go out alone. And I did, drop off Ed and go out with him alone. He aimed me, to the next hotel and in we went. In the room, we fell on the bed. He kissed me hot, I Just melted and for the first time, in my live, I wanted sex real bad and I had, really fulfilling sex, he was not so good looking, red hair a big mouth, a prominent chin, almost colorless blue eyes, not so tall, about 5, feet 8 inches, wide shoulders and small hips, he had a diamond ring on his pinky finger and a gold watch, on his wrist, I would say, he looked less than average. I really liked what he did to me, it was better than anything, I had before. I was thinking that, I won't see him again and wanted to enjoy what I get. We just made lustful noises but said nothing, we just had action and it was so good. After sex we went for Ed and they dropped me off, the only thing he told me was that he was supposed to go to Vienna. When I came home, I sleep until 9 and then I needed to look, after my son. All the time, I was thinking of Walt. Mamma said if the, guys are going to Vienna, she needed some wares for her shooting hall and I could shop for her, she did not have to ask me twice, I was in heat, for the first time in my live. I took the truck and went, where his Parents live. Walt sat there in the sun, I could see him, he was thinking, of me. He was glad I came, he told me to get ready and he will come in 2 hrs for me and so we went. In Vienna we dropped of Ed at his home and then I drove the mini bus. First we went to a restaurant. After dinner, we wasted no time and went strait to my mothers apartment and there we Just fell in the bed, undressing one another, he penetrated me and stayed there and also kept kissing me, we reached a shattering or gasmen and we where not satisfied, ten minutes later, we where fucking as if we had not done it before. Another or gasmen, I don't no how many we had until we fell asleep in each others arms, we could not sleep long and I awaked feeling, his rock hard penis again, moving in to my vagina and we did it again and again, we where not able to stop. Any move he made inside me was so sweet, I can not describe it. We wanted to sleep but the urge to fuck was greater. We came and fell asleep, just to wake after 10 minutes sleep and fuck again, we did not stop at all. They next day he went out, to bring some food for us, I could not wait for him to come back, as soon as we finish eat, we started kissing and fucking again. It was like a drug we both could not stop, we where absolutely, insatiable. For three days and nights we had sex. But then, he talked to me and said he wanted me, to move in with him, he had a girlfriend and broke up with her, because of me. His Sister had already moved her out, of his apartment, well that was news. I did not now what to due, I never now that I could have a sexual desire like this, I had a sleeping volcano inside of me and he had woken up. I no longer wanted to be, whiteout this man and sex, sex was all I wanted. I just wanted his penis, in my vagina and nothing else. I graved raw sex, he was definitely not attractive, but he had some kind, of an animal magnetism and he held me captured. I told him that I have a child and could not live my child, but he said he will take care of the two of us. And so we had another strong bout of sex and hurried to go shop and check in with his sister, he needed fresh clothing.after that we run home to my mothers and had another strong fuck and that was what we both needed. It was so god, I could not miss it. I can not say sex because it was fuck, with a capital F. He said that he wants to stay in my vagina forever and I wanted to just feel his dick, we where like conjoined twins, Just that we where Joined at the privates. We went to my parents and I told them, that I will move in with him. My son was happy when I was back, he was not happy without me and mamma said, 'he acts like, I am a stranger ','"that's because, he is always with me ', I said and I felt very bad to have left him so long. So I left with out regrets, when I was with my parents all I get is food. Daddy was looking out for me, but not my mother. My parents where alone with Billy and Melly again, Rosy was still in Germany. When we reached Walt's apartment it was on second floor and had the toilet outside and no bath, there was running water in the kitchen and a small bedroom next to it and a living room.Very ugly but better than my town house because, Franz was still there. Franz gave me no money and I completely depended on Walt, money wise and sex wise. He had to go back to work, in wiener Prater and the business he and his brother had leased, belonged to one of my cousins, she was very rich. Her grandmother and my grandmother were sisters. She was married to a Dutchman. Erna was her name and my grandmother had send me there to work when I was staying with her, just after my brother died.Walt took me there to meet his brother and sister in law and Erna spotted me immediately. She called Walt and said to him "this is my cousin, dues her mother allow her to be your girlfriend? She will have to call me aunty because I am as old as her Mother.' Erna could smell a rat from a mile away, at the time I did not trust Walt either, but I needed to get laid by him urgently and I did need someone. Walt said yes and all is well. His sister in law was as sweet as they come, but I know this was just for show, to Erna, because Erna was they boss and took no insults to her family. Erna was like a walking time bomb and never took prisoners, She was 50 Years old like my mother and wore a platinum blond wig, her natural hair used to be Jet black and hip length, she had a fringe and that she, died blond and combed it over the wig, so it looked like her own hair, she also had plastic surgery on her slanted chin and mouth, as well as, her long noose and a face lift and eye lift, plus teeth implants. So after all this work She looked dandy, The only natural good thing about her, was her big breast and beautiful décolleté, she had a pot belly and tin legs as well as shoe size 11, but She dressed like a Queen and had always a finger thick gold chain, with a big elephant on it and big diamonds on her ears and hands, actually her hands where very pretty, her best feature, she looked rich and commanding, especially when she arrived in the morning, in her white Cadillac. She was not very close to me, because my mother, always throw Erna out the house, when she came to seek shelter by my grandmother. Erna was poor then, before she met Bobby, who was a Dutch millionaire and he was also good looking, tall and blond curls, blue eyes and he looked like a Royal Prince, nobody could believe her Luck. Mamma said they are together because they swing both ways. Erna had the full command and told anyone what to do, including Bobby. Blood is thicker than water, so the all had to treat me with respect. Next to check on me, was Walt's mother and she would not accept me I know, because I had a child and she was a farmers woman, very crud and cheap, the also treat people like the cows. But more or less I did not care too much, about it. He was a country boy and his family was from an aria where the poorest farmers of Austria came from. Same corner where my daddy grew up. Hard weather, hard people and also they had lots of stupid people there, because they used to give the babies a poppy seed filled cloth, as a pacifier, to make them sleep and that made them stupid. It was very cold in Waldfirtel and for the winter they collected tin twigs all year, they made that to bundles and called it birl. So we call them in Austria birl hacker and poppy seed idiots. This name always gets them of the rocker. They belief I am not good enough for there son. Alto they did not now the fist thing, about a gipsy and I did not tell, they would call me one, but only to my back. Well at least, I was not a farmer's girl, I was satisfied. However they had before owned a small restaurant near where we where staying, the apartment was not his but his mothers apartment. She explained to my little boy. I let her know that I had a nice town house with a garden and we would be soon moving there, I assured her. Walt could cook as well as the rest of the family, because before they get the business with my cousin they where all working in the restaurant, except his oldest sister because she was married to a policeman, who was 17 years her senior and she never had to work just fuck the old man. They had a daughter and two sons the all believed that they where special. I think the where," the where all stupid ". Later I found out, that the innocent red haired daughter of the policeman, fucked with the daddy from the children she was babysitting. But she was considered a nice girl. So they let me feel that I was not wanted and did not belong. Like I was several stations below them, but to me they were below my family. He told me that his sister in law, was a bad girl, when she met his brother and I know from experience that She know every pimp in town, also his brother know every whore in Prater. I soon found out. His oldest brother now was a complete dunce, he delivered bread to supermarkets and once a week he would go gambling, his wife was friendly, but they did not like her either because she had a daughter, before she met the dunce. So when his mother started again, I told her to go and find a Princess for her son, one just like the sister in law who know all pimps. Walt seemed to be ok, but I had no use for his family. I never trusted them and I had reservations about Walt too. He worked long hrs. And wanted to kook when he came home, so I told him, when I am, just home, I do all the house work. He also liked the food I cook and he was happy. When we where together one month, he had a big fest to go with his French fries stand and me and my little boy, as well as his sister went there, with him. The people where we were sleeping also had other small children and the watched my son. It was a big wine fair and the work was a horror, I was on my feet from 9am true to 4 am the next day. So I worked 17 hour, days for ten days. I was exhausted, but I wanted some money for my self and Franz still did not pay child support. So I stood 17 hours bend over the hot oven and still wanted to have sex after. When it was over, it took me two weeks to recover. Finally on the 13th of September I got my divorce hearing. Franz sat outside the court room and he asked, if he dos not agree to divorce me, what I would do? I said; "I will make shore that your home wrecker girlfriend goes to prison, for six months. So you better agree 'I told the court what he did and that he never give me child support ever and spend no time with us and instead of saving money spend it all in night clubs with his girlfriend. I was awarded full custody of my son and get the town house and 15% of His salary that and the part, what the Austrian state gives you monthly, came to 3500 Schilling a month but he did not pay me still. So I did not allow him to pick up my son. I had to resume full time working with Walt because I wanted my own money and fix up my home. One month after the divorce, Franz was supposed to leave the town house. I got the Locks changed before and when I get there with my sister Melanie, he did not want to leave the house and take my TV witch was the only thing I wanted. I said, 'you can not get the TV, everything is mine and if your girl friend want to watch TV tell her to buy a TV."He started to get fresh and I had to beat him with the rolling pin, I hit him on his hand and his watch started to fly away. He said, "You need to by me a new watch, "I said," what about my two gold rings, you stole from me?"At this time we had reached the front door and his mother and brother came, I stood in the hallway and nobody could go past me, I was still holding the rolling pin. His mother said "give him the apartment, he has no place to go ", I said" I got a child by him and got no place either ". And then she said something; I could not believe, she said"If you would not lay down with him, you had no child."After having said so, she charged at me and I lifted the rolling pin to hit her on the head. The Guys pulled her back and I said, "Yes hold you're mammy or she is death". The pulled her clear of the door and I closed it and double looked it. Melanie and I went out the back door and as I sat in the car to start it, his mother came and spit on the window and slammed her fist in the window. Melanie went to her and said "don't do that". His mother was actually frothing, from the mouth and wanted to hit Melanie. Melanie was only fourteen Years old, But a head taller, than my mother in law. Melanie got angry and kicked the woman in her vagina. She started to scream on the top of her lungs and Franz was holding her and the stood by the hood of my Car, so I revved up the motor and said," move with her, or I roll over you both and then we get a free apartment"."Melanie gets in the Car and let's goes!" I said and Melanie Jumped in and we drove off, laughing very loudly, I said," now she can scream when we not there, nobody know why!" After this I started to work any occasion I get I wanted to move in my House, away from the other stupid mother. Walt gave me a gold watch and a diamond ring and he was good to my son, all was well for a wile. End of September we went to a great farmers Oktoberfest in Kärnten, St Veit a der Glan, my family and I had performed there, before my brother died. It was a ten day Oktoberfest and I know most of the carnival people there. Melanie came with us to and I left my son with my parents. We where still in love, or was it lust? The nights where very hot and heavy, I was floating on air when we had sex, but I started to have my nagging doubts, about his drinking habit and his shitty family, but I could no longer imagine live without him. I guess I was hooked on the sex. We had rows and than we made out. No matter how tired we where we always had sex and after we slept like two spoons. He would show me off and take me anywhere with him, but that was mainly because I was driving the car, he had no drivers license and he had no intension to make one, he was to stupid for that, I notice he never read or Wright. All he could Wright was his name. His favorite past time was drinking and gambling, I did not like that. I would drive to the fest 300 kilometer and then he put up the stand, put the gas and the ovens as well as the oil and food, in place and then he was almost, all the time with his friends while I was working. He was a borne pimp and all he did was pimping. I realize that and the doubts got stronger after every fest, I went with him, but I wanted to fix my house and move there with my son. Also I felt that we would have at least, all the material things we need. In winter we where home. He bought a car, a red Opel caravan. He wanted a buffet trailer and my brother Billy build one for us. First a four meter trailer. After that a six meter trailer. In spring I started to work in Wiener Prater and my sister Melanie with me. And we also delivered langos, to other people and went to several fairs and fests, with the trailers and there we sold French fries, burgers, hot dogs and bratwurst.We went to fife big fests and where otherwise Just in the Wiener prater. It was very hard work from April to October. Melanie always worked with us and my son had to be with my parents, when we went on the big fests. Two years after my divorce, I finally got my money from the courts and I told Walt, it is time to move in my house, where we would be Moore comfortable and my son could play in the garden. Previously he had met my uncle Rudy and we often went out with him, uncle Rudy was my mother's brother and he also lived very close to my house and Walt became friends with him. So after I told him, I would move alone and I had the money to fix up the house, he finally agreed to help me and move in with me. It was a lot of work we needed to fix the floors and install a shower and a new toilet; I also get a hot water heater and central heating, wallpaper and rugs as well, as nice Curtains. I made the house very nice looking. I was very happy to move out from his mother. I bought some cheap furniture like a chair set and bedroom furniture. Things where looking up. I had an adopted uncle; He had no family and was a Business Man. He let me practice driving with his car and so I got my drivers license in the beginning. He told me to come by him when I am twenty five years old and he will help me to get a Business license. In order to do your own business, in Austria, that is the Age, you can start your own Business. I went to my uncle in time for my birthday and true to his word, he went with me to get my License. I was very happy, because also a friend of mine and her husband had a big carnival and now I could ply my business with them, they had a 3 day

Fest every week in summer. Walt's brother was the bastard, I know he would be and just told Walt, that he dos no longer work with him and terminated the partnership they had, with out giving him a Penny. His brother gave him the three Fests, but he lost his buffet in the Wiener Prater. I was glad that I had my License and the business was in my name. I believe because of that, he asked me to marry him. Two weeks before we married, we went to St. Veit a der Glan, for the big Fest. Sins he had not to answer, to his brother again, he had started to drink more alcohol. But this time he was very disgusting, at two am we closet the business and I was very tired. When I told him that, I wanted to go to sleep, he told me to wait. When he did not go by 4 AM, I Just left to go to the Hotel. At 5am he pounded on the door and told me to open, or he would break it. As soon as I opened the door he hit me very hard in my face, half of my head went numb. He throws me on the bed and dry to beat me some more. He was so wild, I was afraid; he was going to kill me. Next to my bed where my platform shoes, I picked up one and started to hit him on the head with the shoe and kicked him away with my legs. I beat him good and he gave up after a wile, but he was still cursing me. I just sat in the corner of the room and waited for him to sober up. When he awoke, I told him, that I will not marry him and I want to go home immediately. He said that he is sorry and he will not do that again. My head was numb on one side, I know that my ear drum was damaged and was very angry at Him. He convinced me to stay and after some time we reconciled. Even at this time I know that I made a mistake, when we came back to Vienna, we get married. I did not know what else I could due. This winter, we started to work, on farmer markets they only, last for a day. Most of them where in Waldvirtel, that's where he was borne and we had to get up at three in the morning, in order to reach in time, most of the time there were sleet and fog and I had the trailer hitched on the car. It was very dangerous. I always wonder if I get back home alive. When we reached the marked, he would put everything in place and as soon as he was finished, sit down in the restaurant, playing cards and leave me out in the cold to work, at 4 pm, we would pack up and leave and reach home at about ten in the night. I always made good money but it was never enough, because he gambled and drank regular. By this time I was responsible, by the Finance Ministry and for the social security payments and did not know how to get out of this situation. In summer we went every week to a fest and I was working day and night and he drank day and night. He also played the prince charming with the lady's. I really was feed up with him, but was scared of the consequences, when I throw him out. Also e got along well with my son and I was afraid, to take his daddy away from him, I figure it would be easier when he is older. Boy was I ever wrong with that. I needed a better book keeper, my own was no good, I had some friends, they where Jewelers and I know them true my grandmother, anyhow the recommended me to a book keeper. Her name was Joann and she had a daughter exact the same age as my son. She was very good and helped me save money, right away. I was glad at least some relive. We soon became friends and she always invited me for drinks and to bring my son by her. My tonsils became so bad, the Doctor said you must have surgery, or your kidneys go bad. So I wend to a privet Doctor and she would put me to sleep in surgery, because I could never have anyone go in to my throat, I would throw up. Walt said that I was a hypochondriac. Well I did it anyway. I had surgery in the morning and drove myself home in the afternoon. Walt was not there, as usual. So I called my sister Melanie and she took care of me. In the morning I was paralyzed, I could not lift my arms at all; I had Melanie call the Doctor. The Doctor said that I was throwing up, in surgery, so she had to give me more curare to relax my mussels and this is the reaction. After that I asked my aunt Rosy, she was divorced, to help me out with my son and that was good, she had a good influence on my son and when I was out of town she would sleep over. The next year, I had thyroid surgery, this time I was two weeks in Hospital and my so called husband was not to be seen and my sister Melanie got married the same day, I had surgery. He was a sinty and very lazy, also he was very controlling of Melanie. He was friendly with all of us because I was older than him he had to respect me those are the roles his father was a cousin of my grand father on my mother's side and was after my grandfather's death the sinty leader in Austria. He used to be engaged to my mother when they where children, they where promised to one another by there fathers, but my mother said, no I will not marry a sinty. And that was that. Grandfather, only wanted the best for His youngest daughter, but she was against it. The in-laws of my Sister, where a nice family, but I could not get used to the fact that, she had to obey to all of his family members. I am shore he was at lot better than my shitty husband. One occasion my husband, brought home a friend and both where drunk. The Guy was driving my Car without my consent, Melanie and her husband where by me when the drunks came back and I told the guy to give me my car keys an he get fresh and my brother in law said you can't be fresh with my Sister in law and beat the crap out of him. After that he took the keys away from him. Do not come back here in my sisters house he said, or you will regret it. And with that, he tossed him out, of the house. He also told my husband that he is out of order. I can only appreciate how he stood up for me. The next spring Walt's Brother made up with Walt and rented him a buffet, in wiener Prater. That made him crazy for pride and being with his family made him stronger. Walt brought in some Polish workers, his sister and Ed, had also a crappy restaurant, near by and Walt would go there and get drunk all the time. As usual when I wanted to go home, he did not. One night, I had my son with me, he started kissing and making out with a homosexual, this really got me in a temper and I let him have it, I slammed my fists in his face, the spectacles were flying. Ed came to his rescue and said please leave this Idiot. I left home with my poor little boy, minus Walt. About two days after I found out that I was pregnant. I immediately made a reservation in a privet Hospital to have an abortion. I could not have a baby by a perverted nasty alcoholic. Before the abortion, I had a dentist appointment to go, out of town, with my sisters, about 100 Kilometers from Vienna. In the morning he confronted me again and said, 'you can have the baby, if you can do your work with it.' I said" what makes you think I want a baby from you? You much too stupid and ugly and I don't want one with you at all; I want nothing that ties me to you and your lousy family."He slapped me and I slapped him back, Melanie went in between and broke up the fight and we left. After the dentist I started to have a funny feeling in my stomach and cramping, I dropped Melanie and Rosy off and went home. I started hemorrhaging and went to the bathroom and after I felt a little better and went to sleep. It was the Easter Weekend and he forced me to work. I was so stupid; I stood there with my heavy bleeding, Saturday, Sunday and Monday. Tuesday, I had the appointment in Hospital. They sedated me and when I woke up the Doctor sat by my bed holding my hand and wiping my tears away. He said „I know it al, you told us everything when you, where sleeping, men are pigs, You need to distance yourself from this man, you could have died, you should have come sooner, you already had an infection, because the afterbirth was still in you, but the baby was gone."I could only agree with what he had said, but I also was relieved, that I did not have to kill the baby. Here and then I promised to leave him. Any time I said, that I want a divorce, he would say" but you will have to go to Canada, because I destroy you. You are lucky that I like your pussy or I would have left you a long time ago." I was not scared of that, but I was scared for my son, what would become of him, so I decided to wait till he is Bigger. Not long after that I rented my cousins big buffet down the road, but this was a mistake, I had fifteen polish people to work there and all went terribly wrong.

He went to the clubs with the polish workers every night and fucked the entire polish woman working for me. I could not budge, because I had to work to pay the rent. I wanted out, I was so ashamed to be married to this pig, it was revolting. This stupid hilly Billy treated me like I was his slave, he was afraid of me, but when he was drunk he dried again and again. The only Austrian worker I had there, told me that he is also fucking a hooker every night and pay her big money, for it. I asked him to come to me and ask if I want a coffee, when the whore is waiting, by the back door. And he did, I saw the girl she was taller than me actually by a good margin.I asked her what she is doing here in the kitchen and she said she waits for Adam. I just crab her hair and beat the hell out of her. I made shore to leave the office door open, so he could see me beating her. I beat her so long until I was tired and then throw her out the door. After that I refused to sleep with Walt and beat the stuffing out of him too. I closed the buffet and never went back to prater. I told my cousin to stuff it, she was not happy but who cares. I just went to the weekly fests and where home otherwise. I was very unhappy and there was no telling how long I would be able to put up with this pig. I cried my eyes red every night, I could not belief, and I had a husband such as this. Why could I not find a good man? What was wrong with me? He called me gipsy whore when he was drunk and I beat him so much I was really scared that I could kill him. An ugly stupid farmer's boy and I were not good enough for him.

Aunty rosy got sick and could not help me again. I had a big problem with my son. I took him with me to the fests but this was no good he was all day on the auto droom and I had to force him to go bed and scrub him clean, for a half hour daily. Also he got beat up and I had to defend him. I enrolled him in a privet school, Ronald was very intelligent and he got the place immediately, but he runs away from there, three times. So he was back to public school and the street in the afternoon, or my bookkeeper. Aunty Rose got very ill. I found out, she had lung and bone cancer, we had her at my mothers for three months it was the horror, she suffered terribly, and she did not eat for a long time. I helped my mother as good as I could, but one morning Aunty rose, sit up in bed ,before she could not sit just lay and called my dad, to bring her the shoes, she wanted to go to her mammy. Dad called me and I told him this is the end, people always want to go away when death is on there door. I hurried over by my parents it was terrible, she had a huge hole at the begin of her back it was so deep, I could not believe, because she had wasted away so much, there was no flesh on her. I took the bottle to wash out the hole then filled it with a big amount of antiseptic crème and while I cut of her bloody clothes, told mamma to call the ambulance. I told her to but her arms around my neck and she did what I told her but she appeared to be, stoned she just had he shot of morphine, and then papa slipped a fresh sheet in for her. As we did that a young woman stick her head around the door, I was shaking with stress, when the Doctor said loudly," So what appears to be the matter, with this woman?" You could see she was annoyed, that she had to come. That's when I lost it and said." well it is not her tonsils, it is lung and bone cancer! Aunty rose must have understood me and went stiff. Then the Doctor said, "You should not talk like this."And you should not ask like this!" They carried her out with the sheet so they would not hurt her and when she get to the hospital, she had emergency surgery and they but her in an oxygen tent. When I came to visit she had changed a lot now she was even thinner, just bones and when she saw me she did not want me to touch her, she was afraid of me. I told her I was sorry but it did not help and I did not go back to her. My mother sat on her bedside holding her hand for her last two weeks of life. Aunty Rose Died at the 31 December and it was a blessing, because she had to suffer horrible. Now I had rely lost the only true motherly friend I had, she was always there for me. My book keeper took my son, when I was out of town and I was not so worried about him. The situation with my husband escalated and I was afraid I will kill him one day. One time he just brought me polish people to work on a fest, a drunken costumer, who claimed the Polish guy had, cheated him, preceded to beat me and tire my clothes of me and no one was there to help me, I fought for my live and then, my husband the drunk came and looked at me stupid and said "what is going on?" I said „You are a stupid asshole that is what is going on". The polish guy was hiding and when I saw him I slapped him and my husband. I had to go to court and was fined heavy, because I was an out of Towner, working at a carnival, that is in Austria as if you are a whore or black. I began to heat the World around me. The asshole would not come home for fife days on a stretch and then return and rape me. I started to come down with all sorts of sexual transmitted sicknesses and could not stand it again. I started daydreaming how it would be if I kill him, but what would come of my son, with me in prison? I started to take valium and drink vodka. When ever he came home, I beat him. Then I developed a problem with abscess under my armpit and after having one every week, I could no longer stand it and went for a surgery. The professor said he must make me a skin craft, because I waited to long and the skin is damaged. He will take skin from my upper thighs. I disagreed and told him to stretch the skin from my back. When the wheeled me to the operation, I just know there was something wrong and started a fight with the nurse, so my pressure went up and I would not fall asleep. When we reach the operations rooms, this was so big like a hotel; I called the head nurse and ask her" what operation will I have "? She said both of your armpits, no way!" I said," call the professor and if I fall asleep before I see him, I want no operation". The professor appeared immediately he must have worried, about the money and I told him he cannot do this to me, I have a child, business and no maid to clean my behind witch I could not clean for six months, after this operation. If you wish he said and went in a huff. So he operated only my right armpit. The operation took 7 hours and I awoke vomiting, my right hand was tied to the bed and I could not sit up and also I could not breathe. My roommate saw me struggle to take a breath and was not finding her bell, when she rung it I was almost suffocating in whom it. The nurse came running and cleaned my airways and as I took the first breath, the pain set in and I screamed like a crazy woman. That moment the door opened and my sister Melanie and my husband came in and behind them the doctor. The doctor took it out on them and said don't you see what's going on here and throw them out of the room. He gave me two morphine shots, in each hips and left. The pain eased and I spoke to my visitors, they never came to look for me again. The pain was so strong I could not sleep, so I told the doctor to give me pain killers. „He said" but I cannot sleep either". I said, „But you are a doctor and I am a privet patient and pay us much as in a luxury hotel here and I cannot recuperate with no sleep. „He reluctantly gave me some tablets witch did not help me. The next morning my roommate left and was replaced by an old miserable witch and she wanted the window closed I had to shut down the TV permanently and don't moan when in pain because she wanted to sleep always. My big sister came and we went down in the park, so we could talk, I asked the doctor to but her in a different room. But he refused. My right hand was no good, I cold not stretch it out, I could nor do anything with it, I was handicapped, I wondered if this will get better at all, no one helped me to eat or come my hear or wash up. Rosy and I stayed down there for hours and also went to our cousin rob, who had a business near by. My big sister came every day I had 72 stitches and was supposed to stay twenty one days in the hospital but I could not make it. I again confronted the doctor on Monday and asked him to but the woman in a different room and he refused so I asked to give me some change for the phone and they did not give me. "I said I am going home. " "But you will have to put a signature to a paper in case something happen to you!"He smiled cynical."I said no problem, I am over twenty one."I went to the shop and called my Neighbor from there and told him to get a taxi and come and get me. Then I put one some close, pack up my dings put the TV wire up and when the bitch went to the bathroom, hid her bell. My friend came and I gave him my things and went to the window to close it and pulled the shades down. That made her happy and she said "thanks a lot and all the best to you."And I bend down to her and said, „I hope you croak soon you old bitch!"And I slam the door, so hard, that the walls trembled. Then I run down the stairs, laughing all the way to the taxi. The neighbor and his wife, where very nice to me, they cooked and cleaned for me,

My son was with his friends and my husband was in the whorehouse, no were to be seen, also not my sisters and mother. I was alone, in this world. I told my neighbor, that this cannot continue that she works all day and then when she comes home, she works for me. So I had to learn to take care of my self again. There was a big fest in Villach and the bastard forced me to go there. With my seventy two stitches still in my armpit, I drove 600 km. when I arrived several of the stitches fell out. I went to a Doctor in Villach, she immediately knew the work from Professor M. and she said he always mutilates people like this. The bastard (husband) wanted me to work, but I said "no way and we had huge fights, but I did not work and went shopping instead. I started to put a toy stand, next to my mothers business and made a little money there. Every time he came home I was afraid what will happen next. I looked for a business, where I could get away from him. Moore often, I was ashamed to be married to him and wanted noting else than a divorce. The next year my bookkeeper surprised me that I owed the finance minister, 700.000 Schilling." This can not be "Your husband did not pay taxes for a whole Year, when you where sick she said. But why did you not tell me?" there was something seriously wrong. I spoke to all the government people but nobody offer me help they said that it is my responsibility no matter what. "This is your business." They said. I ground my teeth and preceded working, how will I get rid of him now? "

The child of my soul!

My Son was always riding his bike and for his fourteenth birthday, I bought him a sports bike, but I insisted his dos not drive it on the road. Two summers I had send him on vacation, but it did not work well and when he was in Italy they where starving the children there. Also one of the boys fell and got an infection in his foot and for several weeks we where afraid he would loose his leg. I felt very bad, that I could not go on vacation with my son, I did not want to take another chance and so I left him at home. My bookkeeper kept pestering me to allow my son to go to the new bicycle station, because there is a talent competition. At first I said categorically no. Then after about two weeks, I gave in, the pestering was getting too much, he promised to be very careful on the road and nothing would happen.

I went on the weekend to my parents and but up my toy stand. Ronald went to stay with the bookkeeper, the drunk stayed home, not that I cared. I was going to stay Saturday and return on Sunday home, the weather was hot on Saturday and on Sunday it started to rain a lot, so I packed up my stand to go home. My mother did not like that and said," What are you doing at home?" Remember I got a child there?" He does not need you!" She says."I think he does and I am going!" I said. The traffic was very heavy, most weekenders returned home to Vienna just like me. It was about 1400 hrs when I reached and my husband stopped me in the living room, he was very fearful and he said." don't be afraid, Ronny had an accident but he is fine!" "And where is he?"In his bed, he is fine!"I enter the room and had to hold on to my senses, not to collapse when I see him. He was in bed alright, his head as big as a balloon his eyes huge blisters, puss coming out of his eyes, his nostrils stuffed up with blood and his lips so huge, his mouth wide open and I could see stitches on his lips and puss also on the inside of his mouth. That what I could see from his face the rest was bandaged, like a mummy. He was totally unrecognizable. "I said what is he doing here? He needs to be in hospital! You got no pain? And"

He could not talk and his breathing sounded, „choking". And wile I take his temperature, Walt explains that to me that, Ronny was riding his bike alongside his friend when the front wheel came off and Ronald fell with 60 km per hour on his face on the gravel stone, he had no recollection of the accident, he was seven hours in surgery and the ambulance brought him home at two am and he is fine, also the bookkeeper said that on the phone. Well I said, „The bookkeeper must be a second Uri Geller that she can deter men that, over the phone and you stupid fuck, should have immediately come and get me, because now he has already over a 100 degrees temperature and an infection in his whole head, also he can not breathe or eat. He belongs in the hospital, or he will die." I took the phone and call the ambulance, I put down the phone and proceed to cut the shirt of him and wash his hand they where still dirty from the accident when the doorbell rings and the ambulance was there. That was a miracle, while the dispatcher spoke to me, the ambulance came already. I went with him in the ambulance and the idiot came to. In the Hospital we where rushed into the emergency room and a young Doctor, preceded to take all the stitches out. When he did so the puss spilled out of the wounds. He had so many wounds you could not count them. When the Doctor did this, Ronald was screaming in pain. I said, „This Hospital is responsible, for his condition and if I loose my only child I will blow this Hospital off the ground. This just happened because the Doctors did not do there duty. We got private insurances and I want my child in a private room. „The put he on a drip and on to the stretcher and he were still dirty. I told the nurse to give me a scissors, to cut off the dirty shirt. The nurse said," but you will ruin the shirt!"I said," he needs no shirt, he needs his head." They put him in bed and He had the drip, I made them put up the bars, so he would not fall out of the bed, make them give me a urine bottle and chamomile extract to clean his face. The Idiot said, „We can go home now." "I said you can go, I stay with my child and make shore he is alright". It took me awhile to wash the blood and puss of his face, I just let the chamomile extract drop on to the wounds you could not touch them. I had a towel by his head so the pillow would not get wet and after that I gave him a sponge baht. I left him at four am and took a Taxi home, the idiot was not there, I was relived, I took a shower and called my Sister Melanie, I told her what has happened and that I could not drive I was mentally unable. Melanie came and we went by him. At nine am we arrived at his room but he was not in. The nurse said he was in the ex ray aerie. I saw him, Laing on the stretcher waiting for ex ray, the people staring at him and I pointed him out to Melanie and she almost collapsed to. She said" This is our Ronny? I said yes, please let him not see you reaction."When we approach him, he said that he was already there for two hrs no drink and he need to pee. I had brought a plastic bottle with a small opening where you could drink laying down. Melanie left, to get me some valium, because his bloody face did not allow me to sleep. I sat on his bedside, until eleven pm, I was afraid they could do something to him again, so I always waited till the drip came off. Melanie had separated from her Husband and came to visit with her boy friend. The bookkeeper was sorry for her error and mobilized our Doctor to pull a view strings so all of a sudden I had three professors by his bedside and he arraigned for his moving to clinic Fellinger (where all the Saudis go)as soon as he was able to transport. Ronald looked really horrible a pike of his noose tip was missing; there was a deep gash from his nostril to his lip that's where a front tooth had come true. All his teeth where shaking and the only thing not insured was a round spot the size of a coin on his forehead. Of course he could only eat mashed soft food witch he just sucked in, the sound of his labored breathing drove me nuts. I wondered if he would get well and how would he look? I got him a TV and made all I could to have him comfortable in this hot month of August. My Mother was not even worried; I could not belief how cold she was. She only visited once and that was it. I was thinking she would be shocked to see him so, but it let her totally cold. After three weeks, he was not better and when I come in the room, he had no trip. I was surprised and asked him if the temperature had fallen, he said, "no, but the nurse hurt me so, this morning that I was screaming and when she said she will teach me, how to put the drip, I did not let her put the drip. I was livid and went out to ask for the Doctor. The doctor came fast and with him the nurse. I said "why dos my son, got no drip? Is he better? No, the Doctor said. So he needs the drip to survive? Yes, the Doctor said. Then why dos the nurse has to hurt him so? Is he not hurting enough? First this hospital is responsible for this infection and now the nurse is trying to kill him? I only go home to sleep and when I come back, I see nobody did nothing in his room or for him, I do everything for him, I like to do it, because he is my child, but my insurances pays 3000 per day for this room and the cost of food plus medication and all this woman can do is hurt my son? I mist urge you to keep her away from him. If anything else happen to him here I will press charges against the hospital." He said he was sorry and he will make sure that my son was ok. I felt a little better and when we finally moved him two weeks later an infection was starting again, where the I V was put. At this time we moved him out of this lousy hospital in to clinic Fellinger and he was getting better there by the day. The nurses gave him baths every day and the puss had stopped to flow, he began to look human again, there where still the ugly scars but it was a lot better. He was asking for his daddy al the time and I did not tell him that the daddy was every day in the whore house. So I went to the whore house with a friend and he went in, to get the bastard for me. After I sober him up, I ask him to pretend for a wile, that all is well. Ronald was glad to see him. Just a couple of days, before Ronald was to be coming home, he said to me in the morning, that he had a yellow discharge found on the bed sheets. I know what this meant, I heard that from a friend before and told him to go to the doctor but he said that all is well and he won't. I called the Doctor and told him to make a test with him. The doctor came, to my home and tested him for gonorrhea and the test came positive. I know what this meant and told the doctor to go to court and testify for me because I really needed a divorce immediately. The doctor did not want to testify against him and told him to apologize to me. But he insisted that he is innocent and got this disease on a toilet. The Doctor said "this is impossible the conukous can be only transmitted sexually apologize to your wife". This made no difference to me because I would not have a dirty pig like him in my home again. I warned him not to ever touch me again and when Ronald came home, still kept up pretence. But when the next fest came, I just carried the trailers there for him and stayed home with my son. I gave him one of my friends to work with him and when I pick them up, she said that she won't go again, because he just wanted to have sex with her and bothered her a lot. This was too much for me to bear and I started to go out get drunk and have sex to. It was not making me happy, but I had to do it to get over him, because I still mourned my relationship, but I did not want him again in my live. The big fest came up and he just took my car and trailers and went with his sister plus Ed. In the meantime I hang out with my girlfriend the one he wanted to fuck. I just had a plan and on the last Sunday of the fest, I and my friend took a train to where he was. I know the car would be parked on the hotel parking aria. I took the car went to the gas station and filled the car to the fullest; also I checked oil and water as well as the tires. I parked the car next to the fest, but far enough to make a fast getaway. I explained to my friend to follow me and when I come out of the catering wagon, follow me to where the road made a fork, to take the money bag from me and run as fast as she could and lock herself in the car. As I know he would, he was not in the small trailer, where the money draw was, only his stupid oldest brother. I went in and said howdy, opened the money draw with my key and there it was, a bug shopping bag full with money. His brother started to stutter and said, „What you are doing?" I said what dos it look like? I am taking my money!' "Walt won't like this I need to get him!" That's a good idea I want to see him to, so just show me where he is, I will follow you!" He run out of the trailer, I am behind him he always turning his head if I follow and I said, „Just go I am coming! My friend walking next to me, but he did not know her! I pass her the bag and she run, I still follow him to throw him off for a little wile and then dash across so fast, I just dove in to the people and was gone. She already was in the car and I jumped in looked the doors and start the car, we where gone in seconds. I Drove the car very fast while we both where laughing I did not stop for three hundred kilometers' already had the locks changed on my house and in the next morning, I deposited the money in a new bank account. I had my big sister with me at the house when he came back. He arrived at my door, with his sister and brother in law and when his key did not work, they ring the bell and wanted to be admitted. I told them to take a hike I had already started divorce preceding and they house was mine anyway. They went to the neighbor, I have never talked to and she helps them to call police. The police came and I explained to them, that I took my house back and my business and that his brother in law is driving my car whiteout my consent and that they not allow me to my business and I got to pay taxes for it. I also show them that I filed divorce preceding. The police told them to leave me alone and don't come back to my house or they will be arrested. But I did not get my trailers back. Well at least I had the money and my car und one small trailer. I had to pay for the christkindlmarkt a big sum and started a new company, so I got my freedom from him or so I was thinking. He send me a man, he was the highest judge in Korneuburg, he was oberlandesgerichtsrat and I heard of him, before he was dealing with real, gangsters and let them out of prison, for money. He had a taste for whores, night clubs and restaurants. I know he was dangerous. He told me that he was concerned for me and wanted me to stay with Walt. This was a serious treat, but I told him I will not go back, no matter what. From then on, they slashed my tires every night and they cost 10.000 Schilling. Next it was my electric box and last but not least they poised our beautiful dog. The telephone was ringing hundreds of time a day; I had to get it disconnected. The police said that they cannot help me, if I did not know who did it and they have no time for this. Well I did know, my neighbor who had picked me up, from the hospital, said that Walt was fucking the next door neighbor and she let him sit in her living room. As soon as he see me coming home, he calls the Turkish guy who live behind me and he then he slashes my tires. But he was scared to give witness to the police, I thanked him at least he told me what to look for. I bought me a very sharp and pointed knife and went out in the death of the night and slashed all four tires from the pitch. In the morning when I go out, she was standing next to her car and was crying. "I say wait a moment, they did that to you too? They do that to me every night."From then on nobody slashed my tires again and I came home from the other side and parked my car in a different road. The Christmas marked started and my son and my nice helped me, working there. A number of times, Walt came to the stand with his family and seven of them went in and rob all the daily takings. When I call the police they said I was still married to him and secondly nobody was there. So I wanted to know when the divorce will be they tell me that he has no known address and can not be found. There is a law in Austria that you must have an address or the police lock you up. "I told them that he lives in his mother's apartment, but they did not care that was the judge. In the meantime, I had no money to pay my bills and they bailiffs started to come by me. So I told every one to but the money in there pockets while I was gone, so my niece started to skim money off me too. The next strike was that the police send me a request, to come in for an interview. They wanted to know why I treated Walt and his girlfriend with murder and what kind of pills I take. Walt was trying to put me in the crazy house and then he would be in charge of my business and home, because we where still married and I could rot in the crazy house never see the light of the day again. I heard tat already before, it is really dangerous to get married in Austria, your husband then becomes like a parent. Well that was a good plan. I told my Doctor, that he is trying to put me away. The Doctor said," don't worry just tell them I prescribe this bills and they cannot do a thing to you."I decided to be save and don't trust the Doctor. By the interview the plain close police man asked me about the phone calls to Walt and his girlfriend. I told him that in the divorce court, he stated that he has no address and no telephone, so I could not call him, further I had only 120 pounds, I am no marshal arts and got no weapons, further he has 180 pounds and she about 200 ponds, so what little me could do? Besides that I am happy he is out of my live why would I want to kill him or her? I was grateful to her to take him away from me. So he could not argue with that and asked me, "Do you use tablets?" "Yes" I said. He was happy and started to smile. "What kind of tablets?"He said. "Laxatives!" I said. The word laxatives, had wiped the smile of his face and he said," you may go now. "Auf wiedersehn "I said smiling. He could not put me away, after all, so he started to bribe the people, who where in charge of the fests and when I try to pay for next years fests, I lost the biggest one. The man told me point blank, that because I divorce Walt I get no more place there. This was a blow to me but, I hat to have my freedom from the pig. I had a buffet on a lake in Vienna and I worked there in summer and made 3 fests on the side, so I was able to come down on the taxes. When I was in Wiener Neustadt, on a big fare, he was there with his girlfriend and the big trailer he had stolen from me. As usual he was pretty nasty again. He sat just 15 feet away from my trailer, talking to his millionaire friends and telling them loudly for anyone to hear including me, that he is like a hunting dog and he has my scent in his nose and he will hunt me down and fuck me. Because I still belong to him. I immediately went to his girlfriend. He did the same to her, what he did to me. This gave me great pleasure. She stood alone in the business, while he was out enjoying him self. She was ten years older than him and had big breast like a cow. I said to her," Young woman, would you please tell your boyfriend, to stop molesting me, or I will have to call the police". She was stunned and did not say one word. But the next day I got my freedom, she must have given him hell because I did not see him again. The next big fest I went he was there to, I was really getting tired of this, there was a nice hairdresser, I was there before and when I gave her my name she said but you have an appointment for tomorrow Mrs. I said" no, the appointment is for miss blunderer and she is the girlfriend of mr.h.to whom I am still married to. Most people understood that he was an asshole. But my sister Melanie said that I have a midlife crisis and so did my son, I was pretty hurt by this and the relationship to my sister and son cooled considerable. My son wanted to go to ingeneur school and I enrolled him there he had the second place of 600 boys and his friend was first. After six months I had to take him out of school, because the drunk called him every night and told him, he will kill himself if I do not go back to him. I told my son before, that he was not his father and also let him meet his real father, but this did not help much. The onslaught continued at my home and Ronald was always with my bookkeeper. So I went on a long vacation, to my relatives to Florida. I still had no divorce hearing, after almost three years. America came as a shock to me; the airport was so big and confusing. Florida was nice; the balmy air in the night and it was just beginning of March. They had a nice house, in an aria where all the circus and carnival people lived and also three acres of land. There where the big turtles on the land and poison snakes, one of the trees had a woodpecker living in it. They had orange trees and grapefruit, but most of the land, had a jungle on it. The house had three bedrooms, one for my aunt one for my uncle and one was a shrine to my cousin Helen, who killed herself. I had the motor home for myself and there was also a big trailer where my cousin peppy lived. The next day Uncle Anton took me all over town, to show me the place and to visit with my aunt. She was in hospital having a hip replacement. They said I could stay as long as I want and uncle Tony was planning, for me and my cousins, to go back to circus, but I was not interested in this, they where pretty good to me, but at this time I was not ready to stay in America with no job. We did not know that my relatives could file the papers for a green card for me. I help him tidy up the house and he took me to the circus, he also had a good friend the man they shoot out of the cannon, he was also an older guy just like him. I also met some very good artists they where from Spain and had the new cannon ball number, also they performed on the wire, they where nice and throw a party for us in St. Petersburg. The way to St. Petersburg leads over miles and miles of bridges, just like you see it on TV. It could have been great for me if I stayed there but not with out my brother, I did not want to. When we finish our days work after dinner my uncle sit with me and ask me how all this happened with this guy, it struck me, that he was the only one, I could speak my hind to, so after all he was not as bad as they all said, he immediately took my side, which nobody did back home. After I told him all what happened there, he said in earnest that if I bring the guy to him, he would go to the Everglades with him and the crocodiles would eat him. I grow up with uncle Rudy but when this bastard, called me a gipsy whore, Uncle Rudy was still friends with him, nobody ,included my son took time out for me like my uncle did. I told him that I was really thankful to him for, having my back, but it was to late now. I was no longer able to talk to this bastard. Even when he drove the car, he was always concerned for my safety. If he had to break, he would but his left arm in front of me, because he worried, his seatbelts where not good enough. He was a true Gentleman to me. My uncle really showed me off and I even met the Governor of Florida, they called him big John and he was a friend of my uncle. My oldest cousin who was in Vietnam was also living in Tampa, he owned a restaurant and the youngest one, lived on the same land with his parents, he was working on big productions, like Alexis Zorbas with Antony Quinn. The most talented one was married to an Australian girl, whose parents had a circus and he was running the circus, in Australia. My aunts daughter Harriet was married and working in Las Vegas. Her husband was a bum my uncle said and got in trouble with the mafia and they had to run and hide, so she divorced the bum one time. Nobody had her address. Uncle Anton always said that he wish I was his child, we would be millionaires, then. My cousin peppy had some nice motorboats and took me out on the bayou and to the Gulf of Mexico. That was nice but most of the time I was working on the house. They where like a real family to me, but I missed the European way of life where you go across the road and visit someone. Actually I did not visit anyone in Europe again, because I was finished with them all. But my only son was there. I also went to my mother's youngest brother Willy and his family, he had nice kids and his wife was also nice, but he is somebody, I really do not like. I can't forget my mother, was a year in prison because of him. Anton took me to alligator ally and to Sarasota circus museum, where he also was present. I met a friend of them she is tired trapeze artist and also very good companies. My cousin who had the accident together with my brother was also living in Florida both I never get to see him. There where lots of opportunities to start a new live, but I was not ready. Anton was just like my father drying to find something for me. I also became a new name, he called me Mrs. Clean. I cocked dinner for them and they liked everything I did, I had real nice family there, we played black jack and I won. My cousins felt to me like my own brothers, I still miss them and I regret having ever left Florida. It was a complete chance after this harassment in Europe I had a family where I felt safe and sheltered. Anton took me to Clearwater, it was very beautiful. I was supposed to go back just after the weekend and on Friday before I got a phone call, from my book keeper. She said," I am sorry but your father had an accident and died yesterday."She spared me no detail, Melanie was just before giving birth, to her first child and had to be restrained in hospital because she wanted to see our father. She was not allowed to go to the funeral; it was too dangerous for the baby. When my brother died, Rose was pregnant, it was uncanny. My lazy mother had sent him shopping as usual and fought with him as usual. He went with hi motorbike and passed out, breaking his head on the road, just like my brother. When Melanie reached the hospital he was death and Melanie went berserk, it took several people to restrain her. Melanie was always very fresh, with our parents but apparently she loved them dearly. My uncle and aunt said they where sorry and hugged me, I cried my eyes out and was very sorry that I did not get to tell my father how much I loved him. They wanted to take me to the beach one last time. And so we went, I was feeling treat to go home. But my son was there, if it was not for him, I would have never gone back. The situation there was no good. My Aunt and Uncle were always, making me feel at home. We spend a very good day on the beach, playing Frisbees with my Uncle and cousin. He was always ready to play with us like a Young man, but at the time he was pushing eighty. We had a nice picnic and took some pictures, on the beach. The next day Uncle Anton took me to the Airport, all the cousins where at work and Aunty was still recuperating with her hip. We said our goodbyes and finally, I was sad to go. I wet on the plane to Miami and when we where just leaving Tampa over the water the plane had to turn back, there was a motor failing and we had an emergency landing. But thank good all went smooth. They hustle me all across this big Airport and I had to board one of these little plains to Fort Majors. It was a very pumpy ride. From there a mini bus took us to Miami, where I boarded the plane to Europe with minutes to spare. As I arrived in Vienna, I regret having gone back there. But my son needed me still and I had to attend my father's funeral. My mother was cold as ice and did not shed a tear. There where so many funerals that they had put the funeral for one month after the accident. The funeral was somber and my mother still did not shed a tear. I could not belief; did forty years of marriage not mean anything to her? Of course Rosy did not cry either and neither my brother, but this two I never see crying, I realize they must have had ice in there veins to. The only one who cared was me and my little sister she was home, ready to give birth at any moment. A week after the funeral Joann my bookkeeper asked me to go in her place to Greece with her daughter, for two weeks. First I said I can't my father just died. But then she convinced me to go. She was always looking after my son and her daughter was in need of help. Sunny had a boy friend and when she broke up with him, she could not take it and had a complete, nervous breakdown and did not know who anyone was she was thinking, Melanie was her mother and the doctor was her husband and any time the doctor comes in her room, she would ask him if he comes to make her another child? "I already got seven, so please leave me alone" She was totally out of it and came home in may, knowing again what reality was, but believing she was ugly and stupid, so to get over one man, you need another one. Sunny was a very beautiful girl, very sexy, blond hair, blue eyes and voluptuous. She was 17 years old like my son and she treated me like a girlfriend. I am shore it will not harm your daddy, she said. Ok if this will help I will do it. After I was glad I did, the Austrians are nut funny. A soon as we reached the Air port, we learned that. There was a four hour delay, because there was a high jacking in Athens Airport. There where several passengers from Vienna they where completely drunk by the time we reach Athens. We where supposed to take the aircushion boat, from Athens to Porto Heli. There was this smell in the air, like Balkan; the harbor, for the fishing boats, was very pretty, it was called Piraeus harbor. There where also lots of privet Yachts but our boat had left already. We had to board a bus, to go to our hotel. The drunks were going the same way. The bus went true Athens it was getting dark and we soon came to a rural aria. There was a winding road and the bus drove very fast. The bus driver drove in the middle of the road and in every curve he blows the horn and did not slow down a bit. It was scary. At midnight we came to a gas station and where told we make a break for refreshments. There where 3 small children they started to play catch, while there parents drunk some more alcohol. There where very tall glass doors only one of them open. All of a sudden we hear a loud crash, one of the little children, had hit the glass door with his forehead and the glass door collapsed on top of him. They child had a big cut und they had to carry him to the next hospital. We had to wait there. At two am they came back, the little boy had to stay there. The police man asks for someone to translate English, I was the only one to speak English. The police told me that, the father of the child has to pay for the glass door. The father said he will not pay, because his insurances will pay for it. The police did not accept that and said they will take his passport and he will spend two weeks in Jail. When I tell the man this, he still was not budging. So I said to him," I do not care longer, you are holding up a busload of people and it is 2.30 am in case you do not know, we want to go to sleep and if you want to continue this nonsense go right ahead we go to the hotel only you and the police remain here. All this is your fault you did not watch your little boy!"As I said so, he finally took out his wallet and paid. We reached the hotel at 5 am. And fell in our beds, we had to get up at 9 am, to eat breakfast. The beach was small but nice and the water was so clear you could see the ground, unlike in Florida where the water was murky. I was afraid to swim to the float because I know in deep waters shark like to attack. Sunny and I where very hungry for lunch and as this was going, we did not have enough money with us. The breakfast and dinner was included, lunch we had to buy and drinks in the day. The hotel was very ugly, the rooms where very bare two small beds with white sheets and a small balcony the windows had shatters and there was an ugly bathroom. But they had pretty grounds with lots of flours and a swimming pool, with a bar, where all the drunks hung out. Not once did we swim in the pool. We had to call Sunnis mom to send us some money down and she paid by the hotel with a credit card for a cash advance. Dinner was good and Sunnis aunt and her boyfriend sat with us one the same table, they always eat and hang out at Sunnis home but they did not invite us for a drink. We concluded that they where very cheap. We where not used to this, back home we only drank pink Champaign and eat caviar, salmon and steaks, well we had to make do for two weeks. After dinner we said silently, "fuck you all" and went to our room to freshen up. We went down to the road looking like a million bucks and bum a ride, in 3 minutes flat. We told the guy to bring us to the best disco and so he did. The disco was an outdoor disco and it was like a garden with a platform, where you could dance surrounded by chairs. The owner from the disco immediately took care of us. His name was Adonis and he looked like, a real Greek good, blue eyes and dark blond curly hear and six feet tall. He danced just with me and his friend gave all attention too Sunny. Adonis had a white Citroen and after the disco closed, they took us to Adonis white yacht, by that time we where ready for love. Adonis was a very good lover, I did not have that ever sins I left Walt. We came home at about fife am. At nine we had to get up, or there was no breakfast. When we enter the dining room all heads turned and the woman where staring at us. Obviously they envy us. We did not care, every night I had to go out with Sunny and she had gotten her confidence back. She had a new guy every night. I went home alone, after disco. I found out Adonis was not only gorgeous but also a married man, with four children. Well this was a disaster, with my dream lover. What an asshole. Every night another one would hit on me but, I was not interested, I just had to watch Sunny. After 10 days I had to throw the towel and stay home one night, but Sunny would not. The next day I went with the chef of police to the Ampitheater, for an ancient performance, everybody assured me he would not bother me. He picked me up at the hotel desk, he was an older guy, maybe forty, I was thirty six, I was wearing an Italian dress which was cut as a Greek dress and very sexy, two layers of georgette, with was revealing my legs a lot. But in these days I never managed to go out looking less then gorgeous. He took me to dinner and when we reached the Ampitheater he was bursting with pride. He knew all the police there. The performance was very riveting. After that he asked me to go to a local dance club with him. I did not want to go, but I went anyway. The club was full with people and they used to dance, on a stage next to the musicians. They broke plates on the feet of the dancers, if they dance well. After a wile the Gipsy in me could not hold still and one of the women invited me to dance. Probably she dougt I cannot dance. I went to the stage and danced on the broken plates like a crazy woman they broke a lot of plates on my feet. One of the guys broke the plates on his head. This is the biggest adoration you can get in Greece. When I come back to the table, the chef put his arm around me and his big fingers into my scar on my armpit. I told him for a while to stop but he did not he made me so angry, I slapped him on his hand and get up and leave. It was two in the morning and no people there; the hotel was three kilometers back. A new Mercedes Benz bulled up next to me, I keep on going and he literally beg me to get in the car, I told him I got enough of all this shit and want to go home. He said "get in; I will not do anything to you." I get in the car and say "if you touch me, I break your arm. „He was decent and brings me back to the hotel. He said he will take me to a different beach, in the morning, "I said all right but no fucking around with me. In the morning when I was going out the concierge had my wrap for me, I forget it in the club and the chief of police had brought it for me. The new guy took me to a beach, he seemed very nice and had money, he was looking for a serious relationship, but I told him that I had to go back home and want no relations right now. Sunny in the mean time had wrecked several guys and she felt better than ever. There was a football team going home tomorrow, Sunny said and they had invited is for a party. I did not want to go, but she did not give up, so I went with her, when we want to enter the ballroom two women blocked the door with outstretched arms and "said you cannot enter". I almost fall to the ground, laughing. I said "you really think we want your ugly drunks? Sunny lets go."And we went to dinner. It was about time this vacation was over. It was really getting to me, here where more Viennese low livers than in Vienna. How they always looked at us these stupid bimbos they would have killed us for these ugly stupid men. I never understood how women ken be like slaves to men just for this ugly little penis. I let go of very good looking men and rich ones to. I was abused by two of this species and I wanted no more of it. One of them was waiting in Vienna for me. He could wait long. I wanted no more babies and no more love and abuse. The only woman who was not jealous at me was Sunny; she also wanted to give no more love to a man. Even my Sister Melanie did not want me again. The day we left, we went on the air boat. It was beautiful the Egan see was really turquoise. I saw many dolphins and sometimes sharks. The plane ride home was just and hour and Ronald came to pick us up. My sister Melanie had given birth to a very large baby boy, named Tomas. When I hold him he was very sweet and gorgeous. Melanie was not interested in me and it was a very short visit. I opened the buffet again on the lake but the summer was not so long. I broke up with my boyfriend he was getting on my nerves, he wanted to marry me and have children. He was a rich Arab from Bahrain and wanted me to move there with him. But this was not my desire. End of August, I had a big folklore and wine fest in Krems a der Donau. That is the fest where I went 15 years ago with Walt. I only had a small Trailer, left and went there with my Son and one worker; he was a student from India. My son started to get me on my nerves; he thought that I was an alcoholic. I assured him and so did my mother, so I said ok we are not going out after work and just go to sleep. I used to drink alcohol at times but I never ever could get hooked on alcohol. I just drink it when I am bored out of my scull. Or to numb myself, but it never worked. My favorite cousin, Erika was on the fest to, with her business, she was a real sister to me the only one of my relatives where I could carry my heartache and she knows what a pig Walt was. She took my Son aside and told him about Walt what an ass he is. It helped just a little. My Son did not want to sit with Erika and me, after closing and went with his friends. I sat with Erika and we had a heart to heart. While we where talking there was this tall blond mail, talking like a farmer and wanted to invite us we told him we want no companies." Please leave us alone" Just the twang of his voice was a pain in the ass. We wanted no part of him. Erika and I said good night and went in different direction. When I see the man follow me, I tell him to leave me alone, I was looking to see a police but there was none. When I reach my hotel the big door was looked, but I was scared to take out my key. So again I tell him to leave me alone. But he said in a winy voice."O you don't mean that you want me to come!" he did not budge for about half hour. Than I had enough," I said come with me". He was happy he thought that he can fuck me now. My bathroom was outside so I let him in my bedroom there, was noting of value, the money I had in my bag." I said wait here I got to go to the bathroom. He immediately pull of his clothes, obviously he wanted no shower. I run down the stairs and out the big door and locked it so he could not come out the hotel. I run to my car jumped in and drove myself to Vienna where I had a peaceful sleep. In the morning I meet my mother on the mainline on the grounds. I was taking here to the coffee shop when the stupid guy, started to call my name, which he got from my cousin, calling me that. He was desperate to talk to me. Mamma got furious" What you want from my daughter you bum, get out of here or I call the police, what he want from you? She said to me." Well apparently he wants my pussy I said, but I do not want this farmers boy, as you know I already had one!" mamma made him retreat very quickly. I was glad. The same day, my son wanted to go out. But the other youngsters did not want to go unless I came to. I told him I will not go. So he brought the whole gang to me to beg me. So I just had to go. The disco was full and they music was very loud. But we had fun. I danced with the gang and all of a sudden there was this tall and coffee brown stranger on my side, he was very good looking but he seemed too young. I danced with him anyway, he looked like a boxer and he had a medal around his neck, his hair was styled in a cru cut. He sit down with me and we chatted it turned out he was just one year younger than me and he was a Steal band player from the Caribbean. I wanted to know about him and he told me. He was 36 years old and his name was Emanuel. His parents where not married and his mother died, when he was nine years old. After that his father put Emanuel by different girlfriends to life. When he was 14 years old he had lived with at least ten different families. He had 12 half sisters and brothers and he was the oldest. His father left to seek a job in America and Emanuel started to live by his maternal grandmother. She was good to him and he worked with her on her farm and rode a donkey there. He found a job as a butcher trainee and his grandmother wanted him to continue school, but he was afraid she could die and so he kept his job. Not to long after this the grandmother had to have eye surgery and after surgery became blind. Emanuel looked for her until she died and she left him her small house. He still worked for the supermarket and was in the meantime supervisor. In his free time he played cricket and steel band. He was never married. After I had to tell him about me and we really fell for one another. He was going to be on stage at 2pm the next day. I told him what I did and where my business was. He was very shy, but he asked me if he could spend the night with me. He shared a room with a college. I said why he wants to come with me? They had much prettier woman in the Caribbean. No, he said, he loves me and he would spend the rest of his live with me, if I want him. I really cold not see a future for us, but I wanted him to and strangely I believed every word he said. And then we made love not sex. I could really feel that he loved me, they way he touched me with his soul and I became very sad. He was still here but I missed him already. There was no easy way out. The next day I went to the music stage to see him. He was the tallest and lightest in the big band. They played classical Austrian music and also Glenn Miller. People liked it a lot and they had a very big audience. After the performance he came to look for me and I went with him to my cousin to show him off. She said to hold on, to this one and I was planning to do that, if it was possible. The next day I had to go to Vienna and I took him along. There was no time to show him Vienna. I had to be back to work in Krems, by noon. We spend the last night together and at 9am, he had to go. He had my address and I gave him a picture of me. I had his address and he said he will send me a picture. After two weeks the first letter came along with some nice pictures of him. He said that he was missing me and he hope I will come to see him and if I like it there, I can stay with him permanently. He also said that his eyes where watering when he left. That was basically as I felt sins he gone there was a void in me. I don't know why it has to be like that. In September I finally get a divorce hearing. Walt said that he wants no divorce and he wants me to pay for his attorney. The judge told him, that he could not force him to divorce, but from now on it will be very expensive and he got to pay his own fees. So he said he have to discuss it with his attorney. In the trial break, I concluded that I finally had it with him and if I don't get divorced this very day, I will push him in front of a moving car. I rather am in prison than married to him. When he came back he agreed to divorce, but I had too take the blame for it. I said immediately, that's great, so I do have nothing to do with this drunken whoremonger. I had to go to the big fest in St. Veit an der Glan and when I came there he was there with his girlfriend and started to call me a chipsy whore and said also that is good that the old chipsy is death. I said but he is not going to fill your hole you drunken farmers child. "It never disturbed you that I was a chipsy when you gave me head!" I told him that he was a coward and he could have, never cursed my father, wile he was alive "and next time I see you alone, you get the biggest licks you ever had, together with your stupid girlfriend". The next day the headline was that Dr. Günter Koszick was in Jail, one of the gangsters he let out of jail told of him. He will most likely get ten years prison. That was the judge who helped him everything, if they would have put him away sooner, I could have kept my things. For a moment I was thinking to go to the attorney general but then I did not want to waste my time again who knows, what other crooks he know. Any way the news made me happy. When I came back I was trying to turn the rudder around and get my business better. I started a company in some ones name and rented an apartment, where nobody knows that I was there. On the Christmas marked I cached hell again by the courts and Walt was giving me problems again, one day it was a Sunday I was very busy cooking coffee and tee, I was surrounded by people he appeared and called me one whore after the next. I kept my cool and played like, he is not talking to me.   After six in the afternoon all of a sudden the place was empty, he stood there still, because he was drunk, as a skunk. So I went to him, he did not run, so I lift my left hand as if aim going to slap him and hit him with my right-hand so strong that his teeth where rattling and fire some kicks to his sheen boons.   After that he runs, to his friend's cash ticket box. There I hit him again. His friend was so startled he had his mouth hanging open and he said. "But you can not do that!" I said, but I already did, if you concerned, tell him to stay away from me, or he will rally get hurt. The next day he went to Joanna and let her see his bloody shins. She said she was sorry for him. "This is entirely your problem I said and not mine! I am not sorry at all and if he doth live me alone he will get killed! I got true this lousy period and the wine bar helped me to stay afloat. I did not like this with these drunken yards everybody wanted to marry me, after midnight. It was a drag. After three months the terror started again. Every morning I arrived at the business, the locks where super glued and I could not enter in the business. Everyday I had to call the locksmith to exchange the locks. I was becoming really fed up, the police did nothing and I dry to catch the person who did it but no luck. I know it was Walt but I did not make the connection to my good friend Joann then. But it had to be her, no one else would have known. Too late I found out that I was always stabbed in my back by my girlfriends, even my sisters and my very own mother where zealous at me. I had a friend, he was an airline director and very rich, he wanted me to become his mistress and live in the lap of luxury with him. But I was so naive that I taught I can make it on my own. This was my downfall, the next morning my change was no longer there, he took my waitress and I had to fend for myself again. One morning I arrive with my new waitress and the big window, was stickled up with newspaper, so you could not see what was inside. When we came close, we see that there was an opening in the newspapers and true this opening someone show us a big gun. We turn on heals to go to the police but absolutely nothing happened. Now I was out of the business and after a couple of days when we return we could see there was, no more newspapers and no furniture. So that was it, the drunken bastard still had friends and I had no one. I struggled further with my bills and went to my last fest in October. When I returned home, I found a letter from Emmanuel, saying that he is sorry, but he could not find me, when he was on tourney in Europe because he forgot my address at home. He wanted me to come to him to the Caribbean and stay as long as I like. He promised to take care of me and he also said that I do not need to work. My sister Rose was with me and she wanted to read the letter. She immediately told me "Go, what are you waiting for, to drop dead or what are you doing here, in this shit place, you want the bastards to kill you?" I said "remember I got a son!" He does not need you and if you are dead, you can not help him."I was mulling it over in my head, what she said and I had to set up for the Christmas market begins of November. I spoke to my son and to Joanna and then she said that she will look after my son and I sold the business from after Christmas. The lake was still in my name to further make business and the trailer. I bought a ticket and told Emanuel that I was coming on the eleventh of January. He was very happy about it. I stood in the business together with my son and Rose; it was the worst time of my live, I was not happy to go and live my boy back in Vienna. He was going to get 6000 schilling a month and he had his house and he would eat by Joanna. I was going with two thousand US dollars and two suit cases of close. What will happen to

Ronald and all of a sudden I was afraid to go to a strange man, I did not know him and a strange country. But I been alone for the past 22 Years, ever sins my brother died and I had to start a new live, maybe it would be better. For shore it could not get worse. My sister Rose and Ronald went with me to the airport. A last hug and kisses and I were going to the barrier. I was afraid my heart will brake; I cried and cried until I reached the hotel in London. The very basic room was my refugee. But then I got angry, how I had to Live Vienna, was this the price I had to pay for a little happiness to loose my home and my only child, did I really deserve this? I will show them and I took out my address book and throw it in the pin, just in case, I would like to contact, someone other than my son and vowed never to go back, unless I am rich.

Printed in the United States
by Baker & Taylor Publisher Services